18-
0

WHO'S in BED with the BUTLER?

AN AMERICAN FARCE

BY

MICHAEL PARKER

SAMUEL FRENCH, INC.

45 West 25th Street
NEW YORK 10010
LONDON

7623 Sunset Boulevard
HOLLYWOOD 90046
TORONTO

ISBN 0 573 62970 6 Printed in U.S.A. #25265

IMPORTANT BILLING AND CREDIT REQUIREMENTS

All producers of WHO'S IN BED WITH THE BUTLER? *must* give credit to the Author of the Play in all programs distributed in connection with performances of the Play and in all instances in which the title of the Play appears for purposes of advertising, publicizing or otherwise exploiting the Play and/or a production. The name of the Author *must* appear on a separate line on which no other name appears, immediately following the title, and *must* appear in size of type not less than fifty percent the size of the title type.

Who's in Bed with the Butler?

An American Farce

by

MICHAEL PARKER

was first produced at the

Woodland Opera House

in Woodland, California on August 31st, 2001.

Cast:

Agnes	Elona Benefiel
Clifton	Michael Parker
Susie Legere	Susan Adams
Constance Olden	Sarah R. Cohen
Roy Vance	Micail Buse
William Davis Jr.	Josh Hall
Josephine Sykes	Dawn Spinella
Renee LaFleur	Dawn Spinella
Marjorie Merivale	Dawn Spinella

and

Lora Kennedy

Directed by Jeff Kean

Designed by Donald Zastoupil

CHARACTERS

AGNES (Age 60+): The late Mr. William Olden's housekeeper, she is as deaf as a post and moves about as fast as one! Steadfastly refusing to switch on her hearing aid, she wanders in and out of the action, usually oblivious to the complexities of the plot going on around her. She lives in her own world and spends a great deal of her time looking for her pet rat "Oscar," who seems to be the center of her life. *Likeable, funny, perhaps a little self-centered.*

CLIFTON (Age 40-60): The late Mr. William Olden's butler, and the pivotal character of the play, is a very complex personality. He is not intended to be "pigeonholed" by the audience, who should always be left wondering what facet of his character will be revealed next. He starts out as the loyal servant and appears to be "Mr. Nice Guy," then, as the plot progresses, we see him in turn as the schemer, the scoundrel, the opportunistic embezzler and then, either the naïve lover, or the romantic playboy. (Maybe both!) He is nevertheless an endearing personality with a quick, dry wit and a great sense of humor. Audiences take great delight in seeing him finally "tamed" by Susie Legere at the very end of the play. *Suave, clever, a likeable rogue.*

SUSIE LEGERE (Age 30-45): The actress hired by Clifton to pretend to be his wife in order to protect him from the amorous advances of Renee LaFleur. She throws herself into the role with enthusiasm but quickly discovers all is not what it seems to be. A very determined lady with definite ideas on marriage and morality, she nevertheless allies herself with Clifton, even though she slowly becomes aware of his dubious character. When not leaping on and off furniture to avoid "Oscar" she is at the heart of many of the visual comedic sequences. In the latter stages of the play it is Susie who seizes control and brings order out of chaos. *Bright, perky, quick-witted and resourceful.*

CONSTANCE OLDEN (Age 40-50): Mr. Olden's only child, she has been persuaded by her attorney to contest her father's will. She is somewhat dour and taciturn and would appear to be "all business." As the total incompetence of her attorney Roy Vance and his sidekick William Davis Jr. becomes apparent, we see a softer side of her culminating in a hilarious surprise move in her final scene. *Severe, dowdy, businesslike, yet finally kind and tender.*

ROY VANCE (Any age): Miss Constance's attorney is a "thoroughly nasty piece of work." For him, the law is all about making money and not at all about justice. His frustrations mount as he comes to realize he is up against masterful planners in Clifton and his co-conspirators. Becoming ever more desperate to locate the missing assets of the estate, he seems to lose his sense of reality and becomes rather a tragic figure as he, in turn, makes his final exit. *Scheming, untrustworthy, greedy and malicious.*

WILLIAM DAVIS JR. (Any age): The private detective hired by Roy Vance to investigate the disappearance of certain assets from the estate of the late Mr. Olden. He is one of life's total incompetents who misinterprets every piece of information he receives. He is hit by doors, he is knocked out by a suit of armor, in fact, he is repeatedly rendered unconscious while managing to follow all clues down the totally wrong path. He always leaps (sometimes literally) to the wrong conclusion and, if all this wasn't enough, he clearly spent his entire education studying under Mrs. Malaprop! He is a truly comedic character and such an idiot that audiences cannot help but love him. *Sympathetic, funny, extreme, a natural clown.*

RENEE LaFLEUR (Age 35-40): A voluptuous French beauty who spends the entire play in amorous pursuit of Clifton. She will not be denied and uses all her feminine wiles to this end. She comes close to seducing him on several occasions. She will not take no for an answer and continues her passionate quest no matter what the obstacles. It is only as a result of the determined efforts of Susie that she does not succeed. *Sexy, seductive, determine to the very end.*

JOSEPHINE SYKES (Age 30-45): The second of the three bimbos, she is very English in manner, bearing and accent. She appears at first to be a little "prim and proper" but softens as we see her in her relationship with Clifton. She shows great strength of character when she does not allow herself to be intimidated by Constance and Vance. We feel she has genuine feelings for Clifton and she portrays a sense of sadness when she is finally obliged to reject him. *Pretty, sophisticated, well-educated and articulate.*

MARJORIE MERIVALE (Age 30-45): The quintessential California girl. She takes her affairs with Mr. Olden and Clifton very much in stride. She has a practical, perhaps materialistic, approach to life. As Susie schemes to break up Marjorie's affair with Clifton, we get the feeling that she gives up a little too easily and we are left with the impression that perhaps she was really only in it for the money after all. *Beautiful, athletic, outgoing and calculating.*

SETTING

The action of the play takes place in the wine tasting room of the late Mr. William Olden's mansion, located in the wine country of Northern California.

ACT I

11 am, a Friday morning in summer.

ACT II

The action is continuous.

ACT I

(The curtain rises on an empty set. It is the wine tasting room of a vast Northern California wine country mansion. This room is used mainly for informal entertainment and private wine tastings. It is therefore small, compared to the main reception rooms of the mansion, but tastefully and elegantly furnished.

U.S., rising three steps from the floor level and running the entire length of the room, is an open walkway, which leads off both U.L. and U.R. to the rest of the mansion. Four marble columns separate this walkway from the tasting room. There is a banister railing between the two columns on the R. and another between the two columns on the L. In the center of the U.S. wall about 5 or 6 feet above the columns, is a double door, with carved wooden or elaborate glass panels. These doors, which open onto a courtyard, have fancy brass fixtures on the outside. On each side of these doors is a large, floor to ceiling, window. Just to the L. of the L. window is a free standing coat rack. These windows may have elaborate draperies or lace curtains, but light should show in significantly. D.R. is a door to a powder room, and D.L a recessed bar with wine racks behind it, and two or three stools in front of the counter. The bar top has on it a telephone, a pen holder and a few papers including Clifton's check book, and a small vase of flowers. On the wall L. above the bar is a double hinged door to the kitchen. On the wall R., above the powder room, is an oil painting, which should be some sort of still life, landscape, or perhaps a country cottage scene. U.L. and U.R. are natural wood, louvered double sliding doors. They form an angle with the columns on either side, and match each other. The U.R. door leads to the wine cellar, and to its L. just below the columns is a narrow table with wine glasses, ornate corkscrews, wine racks, etc. The U.L. door leads to an apartment and to its R. is a matching table with flowers, ornaments, bric-a-brac etc. R.C. is a sofa with a coffee table in front of it, and to its L. a low backed easy chair.

The overall impression should be one of wealth and opulence.

Almost immediately the phone on the bar rings. AGNES enters from the kitchen. She is an elderly lady, perhaps 70 or so, and is dressed in a dark skirt and a colored blouse with pockets, in one of which is an old fashioned hearing aid with a wire to her earpiece. She carries a feather duster and proceeds to wander all over the room, casually flicking her duster at anything she comes near. The phone continues to ring, but she ignores it completely.

CLIFTON enters from the kitchen. He is the quintessential butler. Age about 50, he is dressed in dark pants and a vest, a long sleeve white shirt with French cuffs and a black bow tie. He sees AGNES, now R. by the sofa, rolls his eyes heavenward, then quickly picks up the phone.)

CLIFTON. The late Mr. William Olden's residence, Clifton speaking—I see—really?—thank you, goodbye. *(He replaces the phone and turns R.)* Agnes! *(There is no response so he tries again louder.)* Agnes! *(Still no response.)* Oh good grief! *(He crosses R. towards her, she sees him and smiles. When he gets to her he reaches out and moves a switch on her hearing aid.)* Agnes, how many times have I told you, your hearing aid won't work if you don't switch it on.

AGNES. I know that. I just don't like to waste the batteries, and anyway, there wasn't anyone here to listen to.

CLIFTON. *(Sighs.)* Agnes, I've told you before we have plenty of batteries.

AGNES. There you are, the reason we have plenty of batteries is because I don't waste them.

CLIFTON. *(Smiles in a kindly way.)* O.K. have it your way. That was the talent agency on the phone, you remember I told you about them. They're sending someone over, she should be here any minute so *(AGNES has moved L. and, as soon as her back is to CLIFTON, she switches off her hearing aid and continues to dust.)* I think perhaps some coffee would be nice.

AGNES. Who offered me rice?

CLIFTON. *(Eyes heavenward and shouting.)* Coffee please, Agnes.

AGNES. Cover my knees? What on earth are you talking about?

CLIFTON. *(Crosses L. to her, switches on the hearing aid and says quietly.)* Agnes, there'll be visitors here today, would you please make sure the powder room *(He indicates the door D.R.)* is all cleaned up. *(The doorbell rings.)* Oh boy, they're here already. I think coffee right away please, Agnes.

AGNES. You see, you didn't have to shout, all you had to do is ask. Coffee coming right up.

(She moves L. towards the kitchen, takes a quick look over her shoulder to make sure CLIFTON isn't watching, turns off the hearing aid, and exits to the kitchen.)

CLIFTON. *(Goes to the front door.)* O.K. Let's get this show on the road. *(He opens the front door to reveal SUSIE LEGERE. Age perhaps 30-40, she is slender and pretty. She is wearing a pastel colored two-piece linen suit, high heel shoes and hose, with conservative accessories, and carries a purse. She is bright, perky, vivacious and full of energy, and, as we shall see later, a very determined lady with definite views on life in general, and love and marriage in particular.)* You must be Miss Legere. I'm Clifton, please come in.

SUSIE. *(Steps into the room as CLIFTON closes the door.)* Hello, please call me Susie. What a beautiful house.

CLIFTON. Yes, it is isn't it. *(He indicates the couch.)* Please, let's sit down.

SUSIE. *(Sits on the couch.)* How long have you had this place?

CLIFTON. *(Sits on the chair.)* Unfortunately, I don't own it. I'm the butler, I just work here, or at least used to work here. The owner, Mr. Olden, passed away a couple of weeks ago and the future is, how shall I put it, somewhat uncertain.

SUSIE. I see. How long did you work for Mr. Olden?

CLIFTON. Just a little over ten years.

SUSIE. I'm afraid I'm a bit confused. I'm a professional actress, and my agent told me there was an acting job available here.

CLIFTON. That's quite correct miss.

SUSIE. Perhaps you had better tell me about the show. Are you the casting director?

CLIFTON. *(Laughs.)* Good heavens no. I'm the butler. *(SUSIE opens her mouth to say something, but CLIFTON raises a hand to stop her, and continues.)* Perhaps I should try to explain. I mentioned that Mr. Olden had recently passed away. Well, there appears to be some controversy about the will, and a couple of people who are beneficiaries of this will are coming here today.

SUSIE. I really don't see what this has to do with—

CLIFTON. Bear with me please. I should inform you that Mr. Olden was an extremely wealthy man, as I'm sure you have already surmised from your comments about this mansion. His daughter, Constance, who is herself the main beneficiary of the will, is apparently legally contesting some of the other bequests, one of which was to a Miss Renee LaFleur, who, at the request of Miss Constance and her lawyer, is also going to be here today.

SUSIE. And just who is this Renee LaFleur?

CLIFTON. A good question miss. Not to put too fine a point on it, she was, some while ago Mr. Olden's, shall we say, "companion."

SUSIE. I see, this gets interesting.

CLIFTON. Indeed miss. To proceed. Yesterday Miss LaFleur telephoned me and made it quite clear to me that, now that Mr. Olden had departed this mortal world, she intends to pursue vigorously, a new love in her life. Someone she says she has always—er—to use her own words, "had the hots for."

SUSIE. How absolutely fascinating, she sounds like quite a woman.

CLIFTON. Oh, she is indeed miss, quite a woman.

SUSIE. I wonder who the lucky man is.

CLIFTON. That would be me, miss.

SUSIE. *(Laughs.)* You?

CLIFTON. Yes indeed miss. *(SUSIE continues to laugh.)* I really don't see what you find so amusing.

SUSIE. I'm sorry. It's just that most of the men I know, would think they'd died and gone to heaven.

CLIFTON. Oh, I'm afraid she's much too much woman for me. miss.

SUSIE. *(Smiles at him.)* You know, Clifton, you really are a very interesting man.

CLIFTON. Well, thank you, miss.

SUSIE. Now, can we get to the show?

CLIFTON. The show?

SUSIE. The acting job, remember?

CLIFTON. I'm afraid there is no show, miss, *(SUSIE reacts.)* but there is an acting job, and there is a role for you.

SUSIE. I don't understand.

CLIFTON. All day yesterday, after Miss Renee called, I was wracking my brains for a solution to my dilemma, and I decided the answer to my problem was a wife.

SUSIE. What do your mean, the answer to your problem was a wife?

CLIFTON. It's very simple really. If I had a wife, Miss Renee would be—how shall I put this?—discouraged.

SUSIE. Now I'm totally confused

CLIFTON. In a nutshell miss, the role I require you to play is that of my wife.

SUSIE. Now wait a minute—

CLIFTON. This is, I assure you, a totally professional arrangement. You are to play the role of my wife and I am to pay you a fee for your services as an actress.

SUSIE. *(Pauses to think this over.)* I see. Union scale?

CLIFTON. If that's what you require. Do you think you can do it?

SUSIE. Of course I can do it. The question is, how long do I have to do it for?

CLIFTON. Well, as far as I know, just today.

SUSIE. *(Quickly)* The union has a one week minimum.

CLIFTON. Then I suppose I shall have to pay you for one week.

SUSIE. Now let's get this quite clear. You're going to pay me, union scale, for one week, for one day's work?

CLIFTON. If that's what you require miss, yes.

SUSIE. *(Takes a pen and paper out of her purse and writes.)* You've got yourself a wife. *(She adds quickly, looking meaningfully at him.)* For today. Now Mr. Clifton, I want to make it quite clear that I shall expect you to behave like the perfect gentleman that I'm sure you are.

CLIFTON. Of course, miss.

SUSIE. *(Hands him the paper.)* Here, just sign this please.

CLIFTON. What is this?

SUSIE. It's a standard union contract.

CLIFTON. *(Pauses)* Is this necessary? *(SUSIE gives him a "look.")* I see it is. Very well.

(He signs and hands it back to SUSIE.)

SUSIE. *(Hands him a copy.)* Here's your copy. Now just as soon as you write me a check, we're in business.

CLIFTON. Of course. *(CLIFTON goes to the bar L. and sits to write the check. Enter AGNES from the kitchen. She appears to be looking for something as she wanders R. across the room.)* Agnes, I'd like you to met Miss Susie Legere. Susie, this is the housekeeper, Agnes. She knows all about our arrangement.

SUSIE. *(Shakes hands with AGNES.)* I'm pleased to meet you, Agnes.

AGNES. Who are you?

SUSIE. I'm Susie. *(AGNES looks blank. Susie frowns and looks at CLIFTON, but he is busy writing the check.)* I'm the one Clifton hired to play the role of his wife.

AGNES. Hired to stay the whole of his life? Nonsense.

(She turns away and looks under the chair, coffee table, couch, etc.)

CLIFTON. What is it Agnes? *(She ignores him. Now shouting.)* What have you lost?

AGNES. It doesn't matter what it cost. It's not the money.

CLIFTON. *(Crosses R. and hands SUSIE a check. He still has his copy of the contract in his hand.)* Here you are. Don't mind Agnes, she's a little deaf. *(Turns to AGNES, who is now looking behind the chair cushions.)* What are you looking for?

AGNES. Cooking for four? Who are they?

CLIFTON. *(Switches on her hearing aid.)* What are you looking for?

AGNES. Oscar.

CLIFTON. Oh no. Not again.

AGNES. He was in the kitchen a minute ago.

SUSIE. Excuse me, who is Oscar?

CLIFTON. He's Agnes's pet—

(He stops in mid sentence and smiles.)

SUSIE. Pet what?

CLIFTON. Nothing, just pet.

SUSIE. Well what is he?

AGNES. He's my pet rat.

(CLIFTON raises his eyes to the heavens. SUSIE screams and stands on the couch. AGNES continues to search.)

SUSIE. That's it. I'm finished.

CLIFTON. Please, miss.

SUSIE. There's no way I'm staying in a house with a pet rat. Now, please find it so I can leave.

CLIFTON. Please, miss, she'll find him in a minute and then he'll go in his cage. *(He glares at AGNES.)* Won't he, Agnes?

AGNES. He doesn't like his cage.

CLIFTON. Agnes!

AGNES. Alright. He'll go in his cage. Here he is. *(She bends down behind the couch as SUSIE screams again and steps across to the chair.)* Come on, you naughty boy.

(She straightens up cradling "Oscar" in her arms, and exits to the kitchen.)

SUSIE. That's it. I'm outta here!

(She steps down from the chair and heads for the front door.)

CLIFTON. *(Waving the contract.)* I believe we have a contract, miss.

SUSIE. *(Stops and turns D.S.)* You wouldn't.

CLIFTON. I'm sorry about Oscar, but I'm desperate, and yes I would.

SUSIE. *(On the verge of tears.)* But I hate rats.

CLIFTON. He's not going to bother anyone, and, in any event, for an out of work actress, with a week's contract for a few hours work, it seems to me it would be rather foolish of you to leave.

SUSIE. Are you sure she'll keep it in its cage?

CLIFTON. Well, you can never be one hundred percent sure with Agnes, but I'll do my very best. *(There is the sound of a car outside.)*

There's a car. *(He goes up quickly to the R. window.)* Good heavens, they can't be here already. Oh dear, it's Mr. Olden's daughter, Constance, and a gentleman I've never seen before. I had hoped we might have had time to go over a few details, but the curtain is about to go up. *(He looks at SUSIE.)* Please, miss.

SUSIE. The cage?

CLIFTON. The cage. Are you ready?

SUSIE. Ready or not, here comes Mrs. Clifton.

(CLIFTON smiles at her and opens the front door as SUSIE moves D. R. Enter CONNIE OLDEN. She is a rather severe looking middle-aged lady, smartly enough dressed in a dark patterned dress with long sleeves and flat shoes. She is followed by MR. VANCE. Age 40 – 60, he is dressed in a dark business suit, white shirt, blue tie and hat. He carries a briefcase in one hand and a cellular phone in the other. He is a lawyer, who, as we shall see, is not exactly a credit to the legal profession. For him, the law is clearly all about money, not justice.)

CLIFTON. Miss Constance, do come in.

CONNIE. I remember you. You're Clifton.

CLIFTON. That is correct, madam.

(He offers to shake her hand, but she ignores him and moves D.C.)

CONNIE. Clifton, I'd like you to meet my attorney, Mr. Vance.

CLIFTON. *(His hand still out.)* How do you do sir?

VANCE. I'm just fine thank you. *(Instead of shaking hands he places his hat on CLIFTON's outstretched hand and follows CONNIE D.S. CLIFTON shrugs and puts Vance's hat on the coat rack.)* I'll be even better when we find out what the hell happened to Mr. Olden to make him write this cockamamie will.

CLIFTON. Cockamamie will sir?

CONNIE. Let's get into that later shall we. *(She comes D. to*

SUSIE.) I don't believe we've met.

CLIFTON. *(Hurrying D.)* Indeed you have not, madam. May I introduce my wife, Susie.

CONNIE. *(Shakes hands with SUSIE.)* I'm delighted to meet you, Susie. *(She turns to CLIFTON.)* I didn't know you were married, Clifton.

CLIFTON. Well it happened quite recently, and you haven't exactly been a frequent visitor here lately.

CONNIE. Now Clifton, you know I stayed away because my father always had this never ending procession of women living with him.

CLIFTON. I must admit madam, he did rather tend to like long legs and short relationships.

CONNIE. Let's face it, he had the morals of a rutting elephant seal.

CLIFTON. If you say so, madam. Now if you'll excuse me, I need to check on Miss Agnes in the kitchen.

(SUSIE looks desperately at him but he smiles at her and exits to the kitchen.)

CONNIE. Why don't you sit down for a moment.

(CONNIE sits on the couch L. side, SUSIE sits on the couch R. side, and VANCE sits in the chair.)

VANCE. Just how long have you and Clifton been married?

SUSIE. Er—er—not very long.

VANCE. You do know, don't you, Mrs. Clifton, that I have obtained a court order freezing all the assets of this estate, and that nothing can be removed from this mansion without the court's permission?

SUSIE. I really think you ought to be talking to my husband about that.

VANCE. Oh I will, I most certainly will. I just want to make sure you both fully understand the situation.

SUSIE. And what situation is that, Mr. Vance?

VANCE. *(Taking papers out of his briefcase.)* The will, Mrs. Clifton, the will.

SUSIE. What about the will?

CONNIE. Well, these bizarre bequests to these strange women.

SUSIE. I've not had an opportunity to read the will. Perhaps you could tell me about it.

CONNIE. Well, for a start he left his yacht to a Miss Josephine Sykes.

SUSIE. So?

VANCE. It cost over twenty million dollars to build.

SUSIE. Wow!

CONNIE. Then he left his antique car collection to a Miss Marjorie Merivale.

VANCE. This collection was worth over ten million dollars when it was last valued, and that was nearly ten years ago.

CONNIE. And finally he left his art collection to a Miss Renee LaFleur. It wasn't a large number of paintings but it did contain a small Matisse and an early Gauguin.

VANCE. This collection is priceless, heaven only knows what it's worth today.

SUSIE. I'm afraid I really don't see what your problem is.

VANCE. We are contesting these bequests on the grounds that Mr. Olden was mentally incompetent, and we have contracted with the William Davis detective agency for a number of private investigators to assist us. In fact, Mr. Davis himself will be here shortly.

SUSIE. I see. Did Mr. Olden leave—Clif—my husband anything?

CONNIE. No, I'm afraid he didn't.

SUSIE. How odd.

CONNIE. I beg your pardon.

SUSIE. Well he was so generous with these other ladies it just seems a little strange.

VANCE. That's no concern of ours. We have contacted these three—er—"ladies" and we have asked them all to meet us here today in the hopes that we can make some accommodation with them, in order to avoid the necessity of going to court to contest the will.

SUSIE. You mean you want to buy them off.

VANCE. Well, I'd hardly put it in words like that.

SUSIE. Really Mr. Vance, I would have thought you would have put it in words exactly like that.

(Enter AGNES from the kitchen carrying a tray with a coffee pot, cups, saucers, etc. As she comes R., SUSIE stands and looks closely at her. As AGNES places the tray on the coffee table, SUSIE backs away L. above the chair.)

SUSIE. Excuse me. I need to talk to my husband.

(Backing away from AGNES, she exits to the kitchen.
The doorbell rings. CONNIE and VANCE both look at AGNES, who is busy taking the cups and saucers off the tray. The doorbell rings again. AGNES has now finished and, taking the empty tray with her, crosses L. and exits to the kitchen. The doorbell rings again. They both look at the kitchen, no one appears, so CONNIE gets up and, followed by VANCE, goes up to the front door and opens it.
JOSEPHINE SYKES steps into the room. Age perhaps 35 – 45 she is a gorgeous red-head. She is sophisticated and immaculate in appearance. Slender and pretty she looks like a model straight off a fashion-show runway. She is wearing a designer lightweight summer outfit. The dress is form fitting and elegant, with a little bolero jacket, hose and high heels. Her accent is decidedly English.)

JO. Hello, I'm Josephine Sykes, are you Miss Olden?

CONNIE. Yes. Please come in.
JO. Thank you.

(They shake hands.)

CONNIE. This is my attorney, Mr. Vance.
VANCE. *(Shakes hands with JOSEPHINE.)* How do you do?
JO. Is Clifton here?
CONNIE. Yes, of course. He'll be back in a minute, shall we sit down? *(They sit: CONNIE couch R. side. JOSEPHINE couch L. side, VANCE in the chair.)* Would you like some coffee?
JO. Thank you, that would be nice. *(CONNIE pours coffee and they pass cups, etc.)* Perhaps you could tell me what this is all about.
VANCE. Miss Sykes, my fax to you told you that Mr. Olden passed away a couple of weeks ago. What it did not tell you was that the reason we asked you to come here today, was because he left you something in his will.
JO. Really?
CONNIE. You seem surprised.
JO. Well, actually I am. You know it's over six months since Bill and I *(She hesitates briefly.)* parted company.
VANCE. He left you the yacht.
JO. Good heavens. How absolutely spiffing. He always said he would. He named it after me you know.
CONNIE. But your name is Josephine, and the yacht is called "The Big O." *(JOSEPHINE smiles knowingly at her.)* —Oh, I see!
JO. I think we spent our happiest times on that yacht. He always said a boat like that should really be owned by someone whose ancestors came from the greatest seafaring nation history has ever known.
VANCE. It's a wonder he didn't give it to the British navy.
JO. You know, I'm really frightfully touched. Dear old Bill.
VANCE. I wouldn't get too excited if I were you. There's a problem.

JO. What problem?

CONNIE. We're contesting the will on the grounds that my father was not, in fact, of sound mind.

VANCE. However, we do intend to come to some sort of compromise with you.

JO. I think I need to talk to Clifton.

VANCE. Then there's the other problem.

JO. Other problem?

VANCE. We can't find the damn yacht.

JO. What?

CONNIE. We don't know where it is.

JO. It's not at the Bay Yacht Club?

CONNIE. It left there nearly four months ago.

JO. Well you can't just lose it, I mean it's huge.

VANCE. Oh we'll find it alright, don't you worry about that. In the meantime, we are prepared to offer you a substantial sum of money to renounce your rights to the yacht in this will, in order to avoid the unpleasantness of a court hearing into the state of mind of Mr. Olden.

JO. I think I'll need to talk to Clifton about that.

CONNIE. What's Clifton got to do with this?

JO. Well—er—it's just that Clifton and I always got on well together, we always seemed to have a special relationship, and he's the one person in the world I would trust to give me proper advice.

(Vance's cellular phone rings.)

VANCE. Excuse me please.

(He gets up and moves L. toward the bar.)

JO. I'll go and get my things from the car.

(JO exits through the front door.)

VANCE. *(Into the phone.)* Yes, Mr. Davis, you're on your way here? Good. What?—Just give me the gist of it.—I see.—The what corporation?—Are you sure you've got the name right?—Sale price how much?—Wow!—O.K. now listen carefully. I need you to find out how long they owned the yacht, where and when title was transferred, at what price, and above all, who owns this corporation.—Get someone working on it.—I don't care if they have to work all night, and all day and all night again, just do it. – Right, I'll see you shortly. *(He clicks off and turns to CONNIE.)* That was William Davis. They've found the yacht.

CONNIE. And?

VANCE. *(Comes R. and sits in the chair.)* It was sold in Monaco six weeks ago for twenty-two million dollars.

CONNIE. Daddy sold it?

VANCE. Well, yes and no. At the time of the sale it wasn't owned by your father. It was legally owned, and sold by.... *(He pauses.)* I'm afraid you're going to find this hard to believe: The Bimbo Corporation.

CONNIE. The Bimbo Corporation?

VANCE. The Bimbo Corporation.

CONNIE. *(Slowly.)* Well O.K. But if my father had previously sold it to this corporation, where's the money?

VANCE. That's a very good question, Miss Olden.

CONNIE. I might remind you, Mr. Vance, that you are not getting paid on the basis of unanswered questions, and that it was you and your firm that insisted on a fee structure based on 25% of everything you could recover from these three women.

(SUSIE screams in the kitchen. CONNIE and VANCE stand. Enter AGNES from the kitchen. She is on the dead run, or at least as close a woman her age can get to a dead run. She is bending forward and looking at the ground, obviously chasing "Oscar.")

AGNES. Oh you naughty boy, come here.

(She crosses R. U.S. and exits U.R.
Enter CLIFTON from the kitchen. He starts to follow AGNES.)

CONNIE. Ah, Clifton, do you have a moment?

CLIFTON. *(Stops U.R.C., looks despairingly after AGNES, then comes D.)* Very well, madam.

CONNIE. A Miss Josephine Sykes has arrived.

CLIFTON. Miss Josephine! Here today? Oh dear!

CONNIE. Yes, we asked her to come.

CLIFTON. Oh dear!

CONNIE. Clifton, would you please sit down for a moment, we need to talk.

CLIFTON. Very well, madam.

(CONNIE sits on the couch, CLIFTON in the chair, VANCE remains standing above the couch.)

CONNIE. Would you mind if I asked you a couple of questions about my father's er—er—

CLIFTON. *(Helps her.)* Domestic arrangements, madam?

CONNIE. Well, yes.

CLIFTON. I suppose not, you're probably going to find out sooner or later anyway.

VANCE. You're damn right we are.

CONNIE. *(Gives VANCE a withering look, then turns to CLIFTON.)* Just exactly which one was Josephine?

CLIFTON. She was Mr. Olden's favorite from what I like to call his English Period, madam.

CONNIE. English Period?

CLIFTON. A reasonably brief one, madam. One that drew to a close about six months ago.

CONNIE. I see. And Miss Merivale?

CLIFTON. Prior to his English Period, madam. She was from what I like to call his California Girl, or his Tall Period.

CONNIE. I didn't know my father liked tall women.

CLIFTON. I'm not sure he ever saw her upright, madam!

CONNIE. Oh dear. Now I'm almost afraid to ask about Miss LaFleur.

CLIFTON. *(Smiles.)* Ah, the beautiful Miss Renee. *(He sighs, gazes into the distance, then catches himself.)* Er—his French Period, madam.

CONNIE. *(Now resigned to it all.)* French Period?

CLIFTON. About three years prior to his Tall Period, madam. *(Enter JOSEPHINE through the front door. She now carries a small suitcase. CLIFTON gets up and goes U.S. to greet her.)* Miss Josephine, how nice to see you.

(They embrace with a platonic hug.)

JO. Clifton. *(She puts the case down just inside the door.)* I need to talk to you, they're offering me money for the yacht.

VANCE. *(Crosses L. to her.)* Hold on a minute, not any more we're not.

JO. What?

CONNIE. *(Goes up to VANCE.)* Let's not discuss that now. Why don't we go and take a look at the winery. It was always one of my favorite places, and I haven't seen it in years.

VANCE. But—

CONNIE. The winery, I think. We need to discuss Mr. Davis's phone call. *(She takes VANCE by the elbow and propels him out of the front door.)* We'll see you later.

(They exit through the front door.)

JO. *(Flings herself at him.)* Clifton!

CLIFTON. Josephine! *(They kiss passionately. Eventually he breaks away.)* What are you doing here?

JO. That lawyer—he faxed and phoned me yesterday, insisting

that I come here today. I tried to call you last night.

CLIFTON. I see.

JO. Shouldn't I have come?

CLIFTON. No—no, you did fine my dear. I just didn't expect this. How did he find you?

JO. He phoned the yacht club. I'm still a member there and they gave him my apartment number in Monterey.

CLIFTON. This really complicates matters.

JO. Well don't look so disappointed, we'll be able to spend the whole night together.

CLIFTON. You're staying?

JO. Well I'm not driving all the way back today; besides, it's been too long, I can't keep my hands off you.

CLIFTON. Oh Josephine, my little English rose.

(They embrace in a long passionate kiss, interrupted by the appearance of AGNES from U.R. She is again chasing "Oscar." She runs into the kitchen, there is a scream from SUSIE, now minus her suit jacket, who then enters from the kitchen in a great hurry.)

SUSIE. I'm not going in that kitchen again. *(Sees JOSEPHINE.)* Oh, hello.

JO. Hello. *(Pause)* Clifton, aren't you going to introduce us?

CLIFTON. Oh dear! This wasn't supposed to happen. This is—er—er—

SUSIE. *(Helps him out.)* Susie.

CLIFTON. Yes, of course. Susie this is Josephine Sykes.

(They shake hands.)

SUSIE. Oh, you're the yacht.

JO. Yes, that would be me. Who are you?

SUSIE. I'm Clifton's—

CLIFTON. *(Jumps in.)* Maid.

SUSIE. What?

CLIFTON. Maid.

SUSIE. Maid?

CLIFTON. Yes, we hired a maid. We gave her a union contract and now she's the maid. Aren't you, Susie?

SUSIE. *(Slowly.)* Well I suppose I could be.

CLIFTON. Excellent, why don't you get back to your duties in the kitchen.

SUSIE. *(Crosses R. to the front of the couch.)* I told you. I'm not going in the kitchen.

JO. *(Laughs.)* You have a maid who won't go in the kitchen?

CLIFTON. Why don't I find a room for you somewhere?

JO. I think I can find my own way around. *(Picks up her case.)* Perhaps you'd better stay and explain to Susie that maids really do need to go into kitchens. *(She gives him a little kiss full on the lips.)* I'll see you later, gorgeous.

(JO exits U.R.)

SUSIE. *(Comes D. and perches on the L. arm of the chair.)* Why did you tell her I'm the maid?

CLIFTON. *(Comes D.)* Oh dear! Things are getting complicated. You see, she wasn't supposed to be here, and I don't think she would understand about you being my wife.

SUSIE. You mean because you and her are—er—are—

CLIFTON. Exactly miss.

SUSIE. Well you are full of surprises, Clifton; you could have told me you know.

CLIFTON. I'm sorry, there are in fact a number of things I need to tell you, there just really wasn't very much time.

SUSIE. You still want me to be your wife for the—er—French one?

CLIFTON. Miss Renee. Definitely. Now that we've got a minute, there are a few things I should explain to you. *(The front doorbell rings.)* Oh boy. I wonder who this is. *(He goes U. and opens the front door. WILLIAM DAVIS JR. is revealed. He is short, balding, perhaps slightly overweight, but dressed smartly enough in tan pants, dress shoes, shirt and sports coat, but no tie. He has risen to become the head of a well-known West coast detective agency the old fashioned way. He inherited it from his father! He spends a great deal of time, effort and energy trying to impress those around him, always to no avail. It is easily apparent to everyone that he is one of life's hopeless incompetents. He carries a briefcase which is chained to his right wrist, and a rolled up umbrella.)* Good morning.

DAVIS. Good morning. I'm looking for Mr. Vance.

CLIFTON. He's just stepped out. I don't think he'll be long, so why don't you come in.

DAVIS. Thank you. *(As he steps into the room, the handle of his umbrella catches on the rather ornate brass hardware on the door. Instead of simply unhooking it, he prepares to attack the door.)* Hi-ya!

(CLIFTON steps away as DAVIS makes several karate moves with the door as his target. Eventually the umbrella comes free, and CLIFTON places it on the coat rack.)

CLIFTON. I think perhaps you need to tell me who you are.

DAVIS. *(Hands him a card.)* I am William Davis Junior. President and C.E.O. of the William Davis Detective Agency.

CLIFTON. How do you do. *(They attempt to shake hands, but, as Davis raises his right hand, the briefcase swings up almost hitting Clifton, who steps out of the way.)* I'm Clifton. I'm the butler.

SUSIE. You're the company Mr. Vance hired?

DAVIS. Yes, madam, and you are?

SUSIE. I'm—er—er—

(She looks at CLIFTON.)

CLIFTON. She's Mrs. Clifton.

DAVIS. *(Steps in as CLIFTON closes the door.)* I see. Well, as you seem to know, I have been hired by Mr. Vance to invigorate certain suspicious circumstances, concerning the last will and testicles of Mr. William Olden.

CLIFTON. The what?

DAVIS. I should advise you sir, that everybody is under suspicion, and you should therefore be aware that anything you say to me will be automatically recorded in the computer like mechanism within my cranial cavity.

CLIFTON. Your what?

DAVIS. My brain.

SUSIE. I bet you eat a dictionary for breakfast every morning, don't you.

CLIFTON. Perhaps we'd better sit down. There's some coffee if you'd like it. *(Sits in the chair.)*

DAVIS. Thank you.

(He sits on the couch R. side.)

SUSIE. *(Sits to his L. and pours coffee.)* It must be exciting being a detective.

DAVIS. Oh, most of the work is very routine, just occasionally there are moments of great condensation.

SUSIE. What?

DAVIS. Yes, there are many days when I suffer great trials and tributaries.

SUSIE. I see.

CLIFTON. What specifically are you investigating now?

DAVIS. Now, now, Mr. Clifton. You should know better than to ask a question like that. You know I could never foreclose that information.

(As he reaches for a coffee cup with his right hand, the briefcase sweeps several cups off the table and onto the floor.)

CLIFTON. Perhaps I should take your briefcase away from you sir.

(DAVIS slips the chain easily off his wrist and hands it to CLIFTON, who moves L. and puts it behind the bar.)

SUSIE. Why don't you sit down. I'll take care of this.
DAVIS. No, I can get them.

(Enter CONNIE and VANCE through the front door. DAVIS is kneeling on the floor helping SUSIE pick up the cups. As he hears the door open, he starts to straighten up, bumps his head on the underside of the coffee table and, with a groan, falls unconscious to the floor.)

CONNIE. *(Comes D.)* What happened?
VANCE. *(Follows her D.)* Who's this?
CLIFTON. The answer to both questions is William Davis Junior.
CONNIE. Is he hurt?
SUSIE. *(Who has been assisting DAVIS.)* Give me a hand will you. *(They get him on the couch.)* I think he's coming around.
DAVIS. *(Groaning.)* What happened?
SUSIE. You hit your head on the table.
DAVIS. Oh dear. I'm sorry.
CLIFTON. Well, if you're alright, Mrs. Clifton and I have things to do in the kitchen.
SUSIE. Kitchen?
CLIFTON. It's alright, I'll go first. Come on.

(Exit to kitchen followed by SUSIE.)

CONNIE. *(Sits next to DAVIS on the couch.)* Are you sure you're alright?

DAVIS. I'll be fine, thank you.

VANCE. *(Sits in the chair.)* Alright then, anything further on the yacht?

DAVIS. Not yet, but I've got a couple of men working on it, it's just a matter of time before we find it, and this Bimbo Corporation has got to be registered somewhere.

VANCE. Good.

(Enter AGNES from the kitchen. She heads for the wine cellar.)

CONNIE. Agnes, I wonder if you could … *(AGNES, her hearing aid switched off, completely ignores her and exits to the wine cellar.)* … tell me where …. *(She trails off and watches her go.)* She really is a strange one isn't she.

DAVIS. *(Stands.)* Where does that lead to?

CONNIE. The wine cellar.

DAVIS. There's something very strange going on.

VANCE. What do you mean?

DAVIS. Sh! *(He gets up to listen at the wine cellar door. He gently slides the R. door to the L. and puts his head inside, then turns slightly to VANCE and CONNIE.)* Ah ha!

(AGNES enters through the L. door and slides both doors R. This jams DAVIS's head between the doors and the frame. AGNES, carrying a bottle of wine and blissfully unaware of what she has done, crosses L. and exits to the kitchen. DAVIS crumples slowly to the ground.)

CONNIE. Are you alright?

(DAVIS groans.)

VANCE. Come on. *(They get him on his feet.)* He seems to be O.K.

DAVIS. What happened?

CONNIE. Agnes opened the door.

DAVIS. Oh, dear. I am sorry.

CONNIE. How do you feel?

DAVIS. A bit wobbly.

CONNIE. Would you like to lie down?

DAVIS. Yes, I believe I would. Thank you.

CONNIE. Come on. I'll find you a bedroom. Heaven knows there's enough of them.

(DAVIS and CONNIE exit U.R. as the doorbell rings. VANCE opens the door.

RENEE LAFLEUR is standing in the doorway. She is every man's idea of the sensuous French woman. Sexy and voluptuous but not cheap or tawdry in any way. She has short brown hair and is dressed in a low-cut blouse, a straight tailored skirt, hose and high heels. She carries a small, fashionable suitcase which she puts down just inside the front door.)

RENEE. Bonjour. I'm Renee LaFleur. I am looking for a Monsieur Vance.

VANCE. I'm Mr. Vance, please come in. *(They shake hands. VANCE closes the door.)* Shall we sit down?

RENEE. *(Sits on the couch.)* I am burning with the curiosity. After Monsieur William and I broke up, I did not expect to see this house again. By the way, where is my beautiful Clifton? *(She pronounces this C L E E F T O N.)*

VANCE. I beg your pardon?

RENEE. Clifton, is he here?

VANCE. Oh yes, he's here. I expect he'll be in in a minute. In the meantime, I should tell you that I am an attorney representing the interests of Mr. Olden's daughter Constance and I would like to talk to you about his will. *(Enter CONNIE from U.R..)* Ah, here she is now. Miss Olden, this is Miss Renee LaFleur, Mr. Olden's daughter

Constance.

CONNIE. Hello.

RENEE. Enchanté.

(They shake hands and all sit: RENEE couch R. side, CONNIE couch L. side, VANCE in the chair.)

VANCE. I was just telling Miss LaFleur that we would like to talk to her about your father's will.

RENEE. Ah, your father, Monsieur William. What a man! You know he had the most gorgeous eyes.

CONNIE. Yes but—

RENEE. Mais oui—he had that too!

VANCE. Miss LaFleur, you know by now, of course, that Mr. Olden left you his art collection.

RENEE. Mai oui. He always said that paintings by passionate Frenchmen should be owned by passionate French women.

VANCE. *(Gets up and paces a little.)* What you do not know is that we are contesting the will on the grounds of Mr. Olden's mental incompetence, and if we are successful, as I expect we will be, you will, of course, receive nothing. I should also add that we have a temporary restraining order to prevent anyone removing anything from this mansion.

RENEE. Why would you do this terrible thing?

VANCE. Why?

RENEE. You do not have respect for the wishes of Monsieur William?

VANCE. That's beside the point, but we are prepared to make a small accommodation.

RENEE. What is this word "accomodation"?

VANCE. We are prepared to offer you one million dollars to forfeit your rights as a beneficiary of Mr. Olden's will and, of course, avoid the—er—shall we say, uncertainties of a court case.

RENEE. I see.

(There is an awkward pause.)

CONNIE. Well?

RENEE. Well what?

CONNIE. Do you accept the offer?

RENEE. I'm not sure. I will have to ask Clifton and I will, of course, do whatever he tells me.

CONNIE. Why CLEEF *(Catches herself mimicking Renee's accent.)* Clifton?

RENEE. Oh he is so wonderful. I trust him. We have always had this—how do you say in English?—Simpatique?

CONNIE. Alright, let's get Clifton in here. I'll see if I can find him.

(CONNIE exits to the kitchen.
RENEE gets up to look at the painting on the R. wall.)

VANCE. A million dollars is a great deal of money you know.

RENEE. *(Frowns and examines the painting.)* Ah, but I can assure you that Monsieur William was perfectly sane.

VANCE. *(Joins her by the painting.)* That may be your opinion Miss LaFleur, we on the other hand, are prepared to produce a number of witnesses to testify to many instances of bizarre and irrational behavior.

(Enter CLIFTON from the kitchen. He is followed by SUSIE and CONNIE.)

CLIFTON. *(Crossing R.)* Miss Renee, how nice to—

RENEE. *(Turns.)* C L E E F T O N ! *(She comes quickly L. and meets him at the L. end of the couch. She flings her arms around him and spins him around. Her momentum causes him to fall backwards over the L. end of the couch. She ends up on top of him, kissing him in a passionate embrace.)* My beautiful Clifton.

(She kisses him again.)

SUSIE. *(Pulls her off him.)* Excuse me, but that's my husband you're kissing.

RENEE. *(Laughs.)* Your 'usband?

SUSIE. My 'usband.

RENEE. Clifton—married? *(She turns to CLIFTON who has now stood up.)* Clifton, tell me this is not true.

CLIFTON. *(Escapes L. a little and puts his arm around SUSIE.)* Oh yes, it's true, this is my wife, Susie.

VANCE. I hate to interrupt this little scene of domestic tranquility, but don't we have some business to attend to?

RENEE. How can you think of business at a time like this. My heart is broken

CONNIE. Perhaps a million dollars might repair the damage. You remember?

RENEE. *(Slumps down on the couch.)* Well, it might help a little.

VANCE. Mr. Clifton, we have offered Miss LaFleur one million dollars to renounce her rights under the terms of Mr. Olden's will, and she insists on seeking your advice.

CLIFTON. I see, perhaps you could be a little more specific.

VANCE. Of course. *(Sits on the couch R. side, puts his briefcase on his lap and takes out papers.)* I have the documents all prepared. We are to pay Miss LaFleur one million dollars and she is to forfeit all rights to all, art, paintings, originals or reproductions, contained in Mr. Olden's art collection in this mansion.

CLIFTON. Could I see that please. *(He takes the document from VANCE and examines it.)* I see, I see, all artwork in the mansion, good, *(Pauses.)* certified check, good.

VANCE. Well?

CLIFTON. I have absolutely no hesitation in advising Miss LaFleur to sign this document immediately.

VANCE. Excellent.

(He takes the document from CLIFTON and turns to RENEE; he has a pen already in his hand.)

SUSIE. Are you crazy? *(Everyone turns to look at her.)* Heaven knows I'm no art expert, but a Matisse and a Gauguin!

CLIFTON. My—er—wife does not fully understand the complexities of the situation, please sign the document. *(RENEE signs.)* Mr. Clifton, perhaps you would be kind enough to witness the signatures please

(CLIFTON signs.)

SUSIE. You're nuts, you know that.

VANCE. *(Grins at CONNIE.)* Here you are, my dear, a certified check for one million dollars.

RENEE. How about that, Clifton! I am a millionaire. *(She puts the check down her cleavage and moves D.R. a little to look at the painting on the wall.)* You know, I shall miss the Gauguin. It always used to hang here. This is a very nice painting of course, but it is just not the same as the Gauguin.

VANCE. *(Has followed her D.R.)* What is this painting then?

RENEE. I'm sure I don't know. I don't recall ever seeing it before. *(She stands on tip-toe and leans forward to look closely at the painting.)* What is this? I can see numbers behind different colors.

VANCE. *(Looks closely at the painting.)* She's right! This is one of those "paint-by-numbers" things. *(Looking a little nervous now.)* Miss LaFleur, perhaps you could show me where the other paintings are.

RENEE. Of course. The Matisse was always in the library. It's across the courtyard. This way. *(She opens the door. CONNIE exits first, followed by VANCE, who looks suspiciously at CLIFTON. RENEE is the last one out of the door. She stops in the doorway and strikes a sexy pose.)* Ooh-la-la!

(They exit through the front door.)

SUSIE. I bet more men have kissed her than bishops have kissed the Pope's ring.

CLIFTON. You know, you're just here for Renee's benefit, you don't have to get involved in all this.

(He starts putting coffee cups etc. on the tray, but leaves the coffee pot on the table.)

SUSIE. *(Helping him.)* I'm already involved and there's no way we're going to let those two get away with it. Mr. Olden had a perfect right to leave his entire fortune to a cat's home if he wanted to.

CLIFTON. I agree with you of course, but there are things you are not aware of.

SUSIE. Well, I guess you know what you're doing. *(CLIFTON reaches for the tray.)* I've got it. *(She picks up the tray.)* You were right, Renee is quite a woman. *(She heads for the kitchen as CLIFTON straightens cushions etc.)* She doesn't seem to take no for an answer. Heaven knows where you two would have ended up if I hadn't been there.

CLIFTON. Yes, I suppose I should thank you for that. You really are quite a good actress aren't you.

SUSIE Why thank you Clifton.

(SUSIE exits to the kitchen. There is a brief pause then a tremendous crash of dishes falling. SUSIE runs back on stage.)

CLIFTON. What happened?

SUSIE. It's not in its cage.

CLIFTON. Oh good grief! *(Crosses L. and calls in the kitchen door.)* Agnes could I see you for a moment please. *(He holds the door open as AGNES enters. She stands silently just outside the kitchen door.)* Alright, where is he? *(There is no response. CLIFTON snaps his fingers and points to the hearing aid. Agnes switches it on.)* Where is he?

AGNES. He's not bothering anyone.

CLIFTON. Agnes, you agreed to keep him in his cage.

AGNES. I told you. He doesn't like his cage.

CLIFTON. Agnes, where is he?

AGNES. *(Fumbles around feeling for a lump under her blouse.)* He's right here.

(SUSIE screams.)

CLIFTON. Susie my dear, I need to have a serious talk with Agnes; why don't you see what you can do to clean up the kitchen? *(SUSIE exits to the kitchen, side-stepping so as to stay as far away from AGNES as possible.)* Come and sit down for a minute Agnes. I need to talk to you about Oscar.

(He indicates the couch and they both sit. DAVIS enters from U.R. He stops on hearing the word "Oscar," ducks behind the U.R. column and, still visible to the audience, listens.)

AGNES. What about Oscar?

CLIFTON. I explained to you before that Miss Olden owns this house now, and if she knew about Oscar she would have a fit. You know she'd never let him stay here.

AGNES. But Mr. Olden always said Oscar could stay.

CLIFTON. Mr. Olden said a lot of things, but let me assure you that if Miss Olden or Mr. Vance ever found out that Oscar was living in this house, we would all be in a lot of trouble.

(DAVIS reacts.)

AGNES. I don't see why.

CLIFTON. Oh Agnes, you know what he's like, he takes things, he's a thief and you also know he really ought to be locked up. *(DAVIS exits U.R.)* So just make sure no one ever sees him. O.K?

AGNES. If you say so.

CLIFTON. I do say so. Now, the cage please Agnes.

(Enter SUSIE from the kitchen. She comes D.L. to the bar in order to stay as far away from AGNES as possible.)

AGNES. How would you like it if you had to be in a cage all day?

(AGNES exits to the kitchen.)

CLIFTON. *(Goes L. to SUSIE and puts his arm around her.)* I'm sorry about that.

SUSIE. Oh, it's not your fault, I really must try to be more sensible about it.

(Enter VANCE, followed by CONNIE and RENEE, through the front door.)

VANCE. I hate to interrupt another little scene of domestic bliss, but there are no paintings in the library, there are no paintings in the main hall, in fact, there is only one painting in this entire mansion and that *(He points to the painting on the R. wall.)* is it.

(There is a long pause.)

SUSIE. Well we thank you for that little piece of information. I'm sure it's important for us all to know that.

CONNIE. Perhaps Clifton you could tell us where the paintings are?

CLIFTON. The paintings, madam?

CONNIE. Yes, Clifton. The Matisse, the Gauguin and all the others.

CLIFTON. Oh those paintings.

CONNIE. Yes, Clifton, those paintings .

CLIFTON. You'd like to know where they are?

CONNIE. Oh, indeed we would.

CLIFTON. I believe they were shipped to Sotheby's, madam.

CONNIE. They were sold?

CLIFTON. I believe that's what Sotheby's does, Madam.

VANCE. Clifton, you knew there were no paintings in this mansion when you had Miss LaFleur sign that contract.

CLIFTON. May I remind you sir that it was you and not I that had her sign it.

RENEE. *(Flings herself at CLIFTON, who is still D.L. by the bar, and kisses him full on the lips.)* I have a million dollars, I love you my beautiful Clifton.

SUSIE. *(Pushes RENEE to one side and in turn kisses CLIFTON.)* Not nearly as much as I do.

CONNIE. *(Turns to VANCE.)* You stupid cretinous, moronic idiot. You just paid a million dollars for a "by the numbers" painting.

VANCE. We need to get Davis working on this. Where is he?

CONNIE. He's upstairs, lying down.

VANCE. There's something very strange going on here. Miss Olden, could you please get Davis down here. I need to go check on the antique car collection.

(CONNIE exits U.R. VANCE opens the front door as AGNES enters from the kitchen carrying a bucket of cleaning things.)

SUSIE. *(Sees AGNES and hurriedly backs away.)* I'll go with you, Mr. Vance.

(She almost runs out of the front door followed by VANCE.)

CLIFTON. Well Agnes, the fat's in the fire now.

AGNES. Whose hat's on fire?

(Without breaking stride she crosses R. and exits to the powder room.)

RENEE. *(Watches her go then turns to CLIFTON.)* Clifton!

(RENEE kisses him.)

CLIFTON. *(Breaks away.)* Really, Miss Renee, you simply cannot go around kissing me like that.

RENEE *(Advances on him again.)* But Clifton, you are so kissable and so clever, and I have a million dollars for nothing.

(She briefly pulls the check out of her cleavage.)

CLIFTON. Yes, that was rather fun wasn't it? We'll just have to look on that as an unexpected bonus.

RENEE. Everything else, it goes well with you?

CLIFTON. So far, yes.

RENEE. You know, Clifton, *(She takes out the check again.)* I shall share this with you. You and I agreed, everything fifty-fifty, or in my case *(She wiggles her chest.)* forty-forty. Now kiss me my beautiful Clifton.

(Advances on him again.)

CLIFTON. Miss Renee, I have a wife now.

RENEE. Then I shall have to be your lover, and we shall make the love in all kinds of secret places, ooh-la-la!

CLIFTON. You know it is a common belief that butlers and their employer's mistresses should not have sex together.

RENEE. Not in California! *(Now very close to him.)* This wife, this Susie, you shall tell her, no touching, *(She places her hands firmly on his derriere.)* this is mine.

CLIFTON. Oh dear!

RENEE. Now I shall go and find us a room.

CLIFTON. Us?

RENEE. Mais oui. I think perhaps the Wildflower suite. After all, my name is LaFleur and you shall see just how wild I am. Ooh-la-la!

(She picks up her case and exits U.R.)

CLIFTON. *(Comes D. and slumps into the chair.)* It's a hard life.

(Enter CONNIE and DAVIS from U.R.)

DAVIS. Mr. Clifton, just the man I need to see. You and I need to have a little private talk. *(Turns to CONNIE.)* Would you excuse us please?

CONNIE. Certainly. I'll go and join Mr. Vance.

(CONNIE exits through the front door.)

DAVIS. *(Closes the front door and comes D.)* Now Mr. Clifton, let's you and I have a little conservation shall we.

CLIFTON. By all means. What would you like to conserve?

DAVIS. *(Pacing above Clifton's chair.)* What? I mean a little chat about a thief who ought to be locked up. Am I making sense to you?

CLIFTON. Not very much I'm afraid.

DAVIS. So, it's going to be like that is it?

CLIFTON. Like what?

DAVIS. *(Continues to move about the room occasionally looking under chairs, behind furniture, etc.)* Mr. Clifton, I should advise you that I am a highly trained private investigator, and I have obtained information that you are congealing a character in this house. One of criminal dependencies. *(CLIFTON starts to say something, but DAVIS cuts him off.)* Do not ask how I obtain my information, I move in secret ways, no one ever knows exactly where I am.

(At this point he is directly outside and slightly above the powder

room door. AGNES opens the door and flattens him against the wall. She is carrying her bucket and, blissfully unaware of what she has done, smiles at CLIFTON and exits to the kitchen. The powder room door swings slowly D.S. as DAVIS crumples to the floor.)

CLIFTON. *(Goes D.R. to help him to his feet.)* Are you alright, sir?

DAVIS. What happened?

CLIFTON. Someone didn't know exactly where you were. You sure you're O.K.?

DAVIS. I think I'm fine. I seem to have a small confusion on my head.

CLIFTON. You got that right!

(Enter CONNIE, SUSIE and VANCE through the front door. They come D.)

CONNIE. What happened to him?

CLIFTON. Just a slight accident, madam

CONNIE. Again?

VANCE. Mr. Davis, there's no time to lose. I want you to get onto Sotheby's New York office to find out what happened to the William Olden art collection.

DAVIS. Will they know it?

VANCE. They'd better.

DAVIS. I'll get on it right away. *(He turns purposefully to CLIFTON.)* You're not off the hook, Mr. Clifton. Let me assure you that your little centrifuge with the housekeeper has been discovered.

(DAVIS exits U.R.)

VANCE. What did he just say?

CLIFTON. I'm glad you don't know either. I was beginning to think it was just me.

VANCE. And now Clifton, you and I need to have a little talk.

SUSIE. Funny how everyone wants to talk to you isn't it?

CLIFTON. Don't you have things to do?

SUSIE. No.

CONNIE. Why don't we all sit down.

(VANCE and CONNIE sit on the couch. CLIFTON on the chair as SUSIE remains standing above the chair.)

VANCE. A very serious situation has developed, and I'm sure you can shed some light on one or two inexplicable circumstances.

CLIFTON. Inexplicable circumstances?

VANCE. Yes indeed, first we don't find any paintings and now the entire classic car collection has disappeared.

CLIFTON. Ah yes. This may take some time. I think perhaps we might be needing some refreshment. Susie, be an angel and make a fresh pot would you.

(He gets up and hands her the coffee pot.)

SUSIE. In the kitchen?

CLIFTON. Yes.

SUSIE. No.

CLIFTON. What?

SUSIE. *(Slowly and deliberately.)* I don't go in the kitchen.

CLIFTON. Oh, I see. Let me check. Excuse me for a moment, sir.

(He goes L. to the kitchen followed by SUSIE carrying the coffee pot.)

CONNIE. What's her problem with the kitchen?

VANCE. Beats me, you know there's a lot of weird stuff going on around here.

CLIFTON. *(Looks in the kitchen door.)* He's in his cage, it's O.K. *(SUSIE exits to the kitchen and CLIFTON returns R. to his chair.)* Now you were saying?

VANCE. All the cars are gone.

CONNIE. All that's left is an old rusty Volkswagen beetle and Daddy's Rolls Royce.

CLIFTON. That is not technically correct, madam.

CONNIE. What isn't?

CLIFTON. It's not Daddy's, madam.

CONNIE. It most certainly is. I'd know it anywhere.

CLIFTON. Ah, you misunderstand me, madam. It certainly is the same car Mr. Olden used to own.

VANCE. *(Suspiciously.)* And just who owns it now, Clifton?

CLIFTON. That would be me, sir.

VANCE. And just how did you ever make enough money to buy a two-hundred-thousand-dollar Rolls Royce?

CLIFTON. If I remember correctly, it was four sevens, sir.

VANCE. Four sevens? What on earth are you talking about?

CLIFTON. I regret to have to inform you, madam, that your father was not really a very good poker player.

CONNIE. What?

CLIFTON. He had a full house, madam, and rather fell in love with it. He insisted on raising the stakes and finally bet his Rolls Royce.

VANCE. That's incredible!

CLIFTON. I know, I drew three cards to a lousy pair of sevens.

VANCE. Can you prove this?

CLIFTON. I thought perhaps you might ask that, sir. Yes, I do have a bill of sale, signed by Mr. Olden and witnessed by two of the other players. *(With just a hint of a smile.)* Would you like me to get it for you, sir?

VANCE. Later, I'll see it later.

(Enter DAVIS from U.R. He has his cell phone to his ear and waves his other arm excitedly as he comes D.C.)

DAVIS. Yes, good, good work. *(He clicks off the phone.)* I've found the paintings.

CONNIE. Wonderful.

VANCE. Excellent.

DAVIS. But—er—

(He pauses and looks at CLIFTON.)

VANCE. But what?

DAVIS. The information I am about to divulge might be very continental.

CLIFTON. *(Gets up.)* Right, why don't I go and help Susie in the kitchen?

(CLIFTON exits to the kitchen.)

VANCE. Well?

DAVIS. They were sold by Sotheby's for a little over twenty-four million.

CONNIE. Who sold them?

DAVIS. The proceeds accrued to "The Bimbo Corporation."

VANCE. The Bimbo Corporation? This is ridiculous, who owns this Bimbo Corporation?

DAVIS. We're working on it. All we know so far is that it's registered in the Caicos Islands.

VANCE. Alright. Miss Olden, I really think you and I ought to make a thorough inspection of the entire mansion. Heaven only knows what else is missing. What about antique furniture, silver?

CONNIE. Oh Lord! The silver in the main dining hall.

VANCE. Let's go. *(CONNIE and VANCE exit U.L. DAVIS starts looking furtively under cushions, etc. He sees the wine cellar door, leaps away from it with one of his karate moves, then cautiously approaches it as JOSEPHINE enters from U.R. and starts to cross to the kitchen door.)* Miss Sykes, I wonder if I might have a word with you?

JO. O.K.

DAVIS. Won't you please sit down.

JO. Thank you.

(She comes back R. and sits on the couch L. end.)

DAVIS. *(Pacing.)* I need to invigorate the circumstances under which a certain party has established resonance in this abode.

JO. You know, I have absolutely no idea what you just said to me.

DAVIS. I am, of course referring to … *(He pauses and looks around to make sure no one is listening.)* Oscar!

JO. Oh, Oscar.

DAVIS. Ah- ha! I knew it. You know Oscar then?

JO. Well, yes.

DAVIS. Good, good. Let's talk about Oscar shall we?

JO. Why on earth would you want to talk about Oscar?

DAVIS. I'll ask the questions, if you don't mind. *(JO shrugs.)* Now, *(He takes out a notebook and pencil.)* first of all, I'd like his description.

JO. You're nuts, you know that?

DAVIS. Miss Sykes, please don't try to be invasive with your answers. His description please.

JO. Well he's small, brown hair, big teeth, nice friendly eyes and—er—he moves fast.

DAVIS. I see, and his relationship with Miss Agnes?

JO. Oh she adores him.

DAVIS. *(Continues to pace.)* I see, and you?

JO. Well he didn't bother me that much once I'd got used to him.

DAVIS. And do you share Mr. Clifton's feelings that he would be better incinerated?

JO. What?

DAVIS. You know, locked up.

JO. Oh definitely.

DAVIS. Good, very good, I think we're getting somewhere. Do you know where he is now.

JO. Well he could be anywhere, but he usually hangs around the kitchen.

DAVIS. Ah-ha! The kitchen.

(He points R. to the powder room door. JOSEPHINE shakes her head and points L. to the kitchen door. He then does one or two karate moves and moves furtively to the kitchen door. He bends down to listen.)

JO. What are you doing?

DAVIS. I'm initiating certain investigative procedures.

(Enter SUSIE from the kitchen. DAVIS is flattened behind the door. SUSIE moves R. two or three steps then turns and looks L. The door swings slowly shut and DAVIS crumples to the floor.)

SUSIE. Oh dear. What was he doing right by the door?

JO. *(Gets up and comes L.)* Would you believe "initiating certain investigative procedures"?

SUSIE. Well we can't just leave him there.

JO. Can we get him on the couch?

(They struggle to pick him up to move him, but he is too heavy.)

SUSIE. *(Opens the kitchen door and calls in.)* Clifton, could you give us a hand please?

(CLIFTON enters immediately, his sleeves rolled up and a dish towel in his hand.)

CLIFTON. Oh good grief. What happened?
SUSIE. Don't ask.

(CLIFTON and JOSEPHINE get his arms and shoulders. As SUSIE picks up his legs, his pants slide down until they are almost round his ankles. He's seen to be wearing bright yellow boxer shorts. They get him, as best they can, over to the couch, lift him up and flip him onto it, his derriere towards the audience. We now see his shorts have a big smiley face across the rear. They stop and look.)

JO. *(Eventually.)* You know, America never ceases to amaze me.
CLIFTON. How so?
JO. Well can you imagine Prince Charles or the Prime Minister in a pair of those?
CLIFTON. Come to think of it, no, but then I can't imagine *[INSERT A LOCAL POLITICIAN'S NAME]* in them either.
SUSIE. I think he's coming round.

(DAVIS groans, then suddenly leaps to his feet. He looks at everybody looking at him. Finally he looks down, realizes his pants are down round his ankles and bends down to pull them up. They are caught under his feet and he starts to fall. SUSIE tries to help, but he grabs her and they both end up on the couch. CLIFTON helps them up, and DAVIS gets his pants pulled up.)

CLIFTON. Susie my dear, why don't you take Mr. Davis into the kitchen and make him a nice cup of hot tea?

DAVIS. Thank you, that would be terrific. I need a few minutes to regain my exposure.

CLIFTON. *(At this point CLIFTON leans forward to stare directly at Davis's zipper which he is about to pull up.)* What?

SUSIE. Don't ask. Come along, Mr. Davis.

(DAVIS takes a step or two to his L. towards the kitchen but bumps his knee on the arm of the chair. He leaps back and strikes a karate pose, then catches himself and smiles at everybody.)

CLIFTON. I'll get the door for you.

SUSIE. Thank you.

(CLIFTON goes L. and holds open the kitchen door. SUSIE and DAVIS exit to the kitchen. JOSEPHINE, who has followed them all L., strikes a sexy pose by the U.L. table.)

CLIFTON. *(Turns from the kitchen door.)* My God Josephine, you look ravishing.

JO. Well, why don't you ravish me then? *(They kiss passionately.)* Give me five minutes.

(VANCE and CONNIE appear U.L. As they come D., they see CLIFTON embracing someone, but he has turned so his back is towards them and JOSEPHINE is partially hidden from their view. Reaching behind JOSEPHINE's back, CLIFTON slides open the apartment door and quickly pushes her inside. Sliding the door almost closed he stands with his back to it. JOSEPHINE's arm immediately reappears [SEE AUTHOR'S NOTES] as VANCE and CONNIE come down the steps. During the following conversation JOSEPHINE's arm is visible through the open door. CLIFTON twice tries to remove it, but

each time it returns, so he quickly tucks his own right arm behind his back so JOSEPHINE's arm appears to be his. JOSEPHINE's right hand now draws circles on his chest. His eyes grow ever wider as the hand moves down, perilously close to forbidden territory, watched most of the time by CONNIE and VANCE.)

CONNIE. Please don't be embarrassed Clifton, it's not a crime to be caught kissing your wife you know.

CLIFTON. Ah yes! My wife, yes!

(He looks nervously at the kitchen door.)

CONNIE. Perhaps she'd care to join us in a glass of wine?

CLIFTON. Do you think there'd be room?

CONNIE. What?

CLIFTON. I'm sorry, I couldn't resist that.

CONNIE. Mr. Vance tells me he has a number of things he'd like to discuss with you.

VANCE. *(Crossing R. behind the couch to the U.R. table.)* You're dead right about that.

(CONNIE turns to go R. CLIFTON tries to follow but the arm is now locked around his neck and turns him around so his head is half in the closet. Only a little of JOSEPHINE's hair is visible as she kisses him long and hard on the lips. CLIFTON has made a little noise of protest and, as this happens, CONNIE comes back L. to watch.)

CONNIE. I do believe your wife is trying to tell you something Clifton.

(CLIFTON, still locked in the embrace, struggles feebly.)

VANCE. *(Pouring wine at the table U.R.)* Let's all sit down together and discuss the disappearance of all these assets, like reasonable people.

(CONNIE turns R. and moves to the couch as SUSIE enters from the kitchen. Neither VANCE, who is busy pouring wine, nor CONNIE who has her back to her, sees SUSIE enter. CLIFTON finally breaks loose from "the arm," grabs SUSIE and kisses her. CONNIE sees this.)

CLIFTON. *(Breaks the embrace.)* Susie dear, this is hardly the time, and we do have guests.

SUSIE. What?

(During the following conversation "the arm" remains visible at all times. Glimpses of legs, shoulders, hair, etc., can also be seen in the entrance to Clifton's apartment. First the bolero jacket, then the dress shoes, hose and underwear are slowly and seductively peeled off and thrown off stage into the apartment.)

CLIFTON. Mr. Vance and Miss Olden have invited us to join them in a glass of wine.

SUSIE. Don't you think it would be a little crowded?

CLIFTON. We've already done that.

SUSIE. We have?

CLIFTON. I really do apologize madam. I'm afraid my wife and I got a little carried away.

SUSIE. We did? What did we do?

CONNIE. Don't apologize, Clifton, there's really nothing wrong with a little "love in the afternoon."

(CONNIE sits on the couch R. end, Susie on the couch L. end. CLIFTON sits in the chair, continuously looking over his left

shoulder at what is going on in the doorway to the apartment. VANCE hands a glass of wine to CONNIE and SUSIE, but pointedly not CLIFTON, and remains standing behind the couch.)

CLIFTON. Thank you, madam, it's just that, you know, we haven't been married very long.

VANCE. Really? That's very interesting. Just how long have you been married?

(CLIFTON and SUSIE look at each other.)

CLIFTON. Three weeks. SUSIE. Three months.

(There is a brief pause.)

CLIFTON. Three months. SUSIE. Three weeks.

CLIFTON. Three months, three weeks and how many days, my love?

SUSIE. *(Smiles.)* Who's counting?

VANCE. Let's get back to the cars shall we? Are you telling me that all that's left of a collection of over one hundred antique and classic cars is a rusting old Volkswagen beetle?

CLIFTON. *(With just a hint of a smile.)* It certainly looks that way, sir.

VANCE. Cut the crap, Clifton. What the hell happened to the cars?

CLIFTON. I believe they were disposed of a little over a year ago, sir.

CONNIE. They were sold?

CLIFTON. I believe so madam.

CONNIE. Then where's the money?

CLIFTON. I do believe Mr. Olden transferred ownership of the car collection to a limited liability company, and I imagine the proceeds of the sale accrued to that corporation.

VANCE. You wouldn't happen to know the name of that corporation would you, Clifton?

(Enter AGNES from the kitchen. She is once again chasing "Oscar." She comes R. and reaches down behind Clifton's chair as SUSIE screams and stands on the couch. AGNES straightens up cradling "Oscar" in her arms and heads U.L.)

SUSIE. You promised me.

CLIFTON. *(On his feet.)* Agnes! *(She continues U.L. CLIFTON moves U.L. to the columns and shouts.)* Agnes! *(She stops and turns.)* Lock him up.

AGNES. Get you own cup. I'm busy.

(AGNES exits U.L.
At this point the "arm" twists around what must be the last article of clothing; it is a bra which is now thrown D.S. Clifton catches it, moves smoothly to the apartment door and hands the bra back to the "arm.")

CLIFTON. I'll be in, in a minute. *(He closes the apartment door, moves R. to SUSIE and helps her down.)* It's alright dear, maybe you should join Mr. Davis with a nice cup of hot tea yourself. Excuse us for a moment please madam.

(CLIFTON and SUSIE exit to the kitchen.)

CONNIE. What was all that about?

VANCE. Have you noticed how you never get to the end of a conversation with Clifton?

(The doorbell rings. They look briefly at the kitchen door, then

CONNIE goes up to open it.
MARJORIE MERIVALE steps into the room. She is the epitome of "The California Girl," tall and slender with long blonde hair and a generous bosom. She is wearing a halter top, showing a bare midriff, a very short skirt and flat white sandals. She carries a small overnight case.)

MARJORIE. Hello. I'm Marjorie Merivale.

CONNIE. Please come in, I'm Connie Olden and this is my attorney, Mr. Vance.

(They shake hands.)

VANCE. How do you do?

MARJORIE. Hello, is Clifton still here?

CONNIE. Oh yes, I expect he'll be in in a minute. Why don't we sit down.

(MARJORIE leaves her case by the front door. CONNIE sits on the couch. MARJORIE sits in the chair, VANCE remains standing above the chair.)

MARJORIE. Thank you. *(There is a brief awkward moment.)* So, you gonna tell me why I'm here?

VANCE. At the moment that's a kind of moot point. We asked you to come here because Mr. Olden left you his entire antique car collection in his will, worth, as I'm sure you know, several million dollars, but we can't find it.

MARJORIE. I beg your pardon.

VANCE. It's not here.

MARJORIE. He left me all those cars?

CONNIE. You didn't know

MARJORIE. I had no idea. I mean he always used to kind of joke about it, and say he would leave them to me, but I never took him seriously.

CONNIE. Well, he did.

MARJORIE. You know what he used to say? He said classic beauty like the cars deserved to be owned by a classic beauty like me, but it was kind of, like a joke.

VANCE. Miss Merivale, we asked you to come here today because we are contesting some of the bequests in Mr. Olden's will, but until we find out what happened to the cars, we really don't have any firm proposal to make to you.

MARJORIE. Proposal?

VANCE. We intended to make you an offer for the cars.

MARJORIE. I think I need to talk to Clifton.

(Enter AGNES from U.L. cradling "Oscar" in her arms.)

VANCE. Agnes, I wonder if I could have a word with you?

(AGNES, her hearing aid switched off, ignores him and exits to the kitchen. There is a huge scream from SUSIE and everyone is on their feet as she enters and runs R. across the stage followed by CLIFTON.)

CONNIE. Mrs. Clifton!

(SUSIE runs into the powder room and slams the door. CLIFTON has been followed out of the kitchen door by DAVIS, but, as CLIFTON lets go of the kitchen door, it swings shut to hit DAVIS in the doorway. CLIFTON follows SUSIE to the powder room as DAVIS goes down unconscious in the doorway.)

CLIFTON. *(Outside the powder room door.)* Susie. Oh Susie, it's alright.

(He turns U.S.)

MARJORIE. *(Comes D.R.)* Clifton, how nice to see you.

(They give each other a platonic hug.)

CLIFTON. Oh dear!
MARJORIE. What?
CLIFTON. I didn't know you were coming here today.
MARJORIE. *(Shrugs.)* Well, they asked me to.
CLIFTON. Oh dear!
MARJORIE. There's some sort of problem?
CLIFTON. Well—er—

(He nods to CONNIE and VANCE.)

CONNIE. *(Moving L. to look at DAVIS on the floor in the kitchen doorway.)* Do you suppose we should do something with him?
VANCE. *(Has followed her L.)* He'll probably get into less trouble if we leave him where he is.
CONNIE. We can't just leave him there.
VANCE. Alright, come on, give me a hand.

(They drag him and exit to the kitchen. CLIFTON and MARJORIE look to make sure they've gone. Then:)

CLIFTON and MARJORIE. *(Together)* Darling!

(They kiss passionately.)

MARJORIE. It's been too long. I can't keep my hands off you.

(They kiss again.)

CLIFTON. *(Breaks away and looks nervously around.)* You're not supposed to be here.

MARJORIE. I know, but they faxed me yesterday. I tried to call you last night. Anyway it doesn't matter, we get to stay together and spend the night in your apartment.

(She starts to move U.L.)

CLIFTON. *(Runs to stop her.)* You can't do that

MARJORIE. I most certainly can.

CLIFTON. No. I—er—er—I don't live there anymore.

MARJORIE. Oh!

CLIFTON. Yes, after Mr. Olden died, I had the house to myself and I moved to er—er—the Rose Room.

MARJORIE. Way to go Clifton, come on then. *(She heads up the steps and picks up her case as SUSIE opens the door of the powder room and watches. As they get to the extreme R. column she drops the case and grabs him.)* Clifton, you gorgeous beast, you're mine, all mine.

(She kisses him by the column. As they embrace CLIFTON's back is visible to the audience but only MARJORIE's hair, her face hidden from view. SUSIE steps out on the stage as the curtain falls.).

ACT II

(The action is continuous. [SEE AUTHOR'S NOTE])

CLIFTON. I'll see you in the Rose Room in a few minutes.

("MARJORIE" exits U.R.; CLIFTON comes D. and heads L. to the kitchen as SUSIE watches from the powder room. JOSEPHINE enters from the apartment; she appears to be wearing nothing but a sheet wrapped around her.)

JO. *(Advances on CLIFTON and puts her arms around his neck.)* Come on lover boy, it's been too long.

CLIFTON. *(Looking nervously around.)* Oh dear, things have got rather complicated.

JO. Well, why don't you let me uncomplicate them.

(She kisses him.)

CLIFTON. *(Eventually.)* Oh Josephine, my little English rose. What am I to do?

JO. Oh, I think you know what to do!

CLIFTON. Give me two minutes. I've just got a couple of things to do. I'll be in in two minutes.

JO. Alright. Two minutes. If you're not in that bed in two minutes, I'm coming to get you.

(She goes back into the apartment and CLIFTON slides the door shut.)

SUSIE. *(Comes slowly U.C.)* Well, well, you really are a busy boy aren't you?
CLIFTON. Oh dear, I can explain.
SUSIE. I can't wait to hear this.
CLIFTON. Well, you see—

(Enter CONNIE and VANCE from the kitchen.)

VANCE. We need to talk to you, Clifton.
CLIFTON. Oh dear, I was afraid you were going to say that.
CONNIE. Let's all sit down shall we?

(They all cross R., CONNIE and VANCE go to the couch. CLIFTON heads towards the chair. SUSIE just stands there.)

CLIFTON. Susie my dear, we'll be serving lunch in here shortly. I've started on the lunch trolley, perhaps you could finish it for me. You'll find everything on the counter and in the fridge.
SUSIE. I've told you, I'm not going in the kitchen.
CLIFTON. Oh, yes—er—

(Enter AGNES from the kitchen. She crosses to go U.R. as SUSIE moves to keep away from her.)

CLIFTON. Agnes, is it safe in there?
AGNES. Wave my hair. Mind your own business.

(AGNES exits U.R.)

CONNIE. She does seem a bit superfluous doesn't she?

CLIFTON. I'll just check the kitchen. *(He looks in the kitchen door.)* It's alright.

SUSIE. You sure?

(SUSIE picks up the two wine glasses from the coffee table.)

CLIFTON. Yes, would you please finish the lunch trolley?

SUSIE. *(Hesitates by the kitchen door.)* Are you sure? *(Clifton gives her "a look.")* O.K. O.K.

(SUSIE exits to kitchen. CLIFTON has been holding the kitchen door open for SUSIE. As she exits he turns, but the sliding door to the apartment opens, he is grabbed by JOSEPHINE's [SEE AUTHOR'S NOTE] arm and pulled inside. The sliding door glides silently shut.)

CONNIE. *(Looks L.)* Now where's he gone?

VANCE. *(On his feet.)* He's done it again. Every time I try to talk to him he disappears.

CONNIE. Do you suppose he has anything to do with this Bimbo Corporation? *(Enter RENEE from U.L.)* And talking of bimbos, here comes another one.

RENEE. *(Comes D.C.)* This mountain air, it makes me so hungry. Is Clifton in the kitchen?

VANCE. We're not quite sure where he is.

CONNIE. However, I believe Mrs. Clifton is preparing lunch right now.

RENEE. Bon. Madame, would you mind if I got a bottle of wine from the cellar for us to have with lunch?

CONNIE. Not at all. In fact, that would be nice.

RENEE. Merci. Thank you very much, the wine cellar was—

(She hesitates.)

CONNIE. Yes?

RENEE. Nothing, it was just one of our favorite places for—er—excusez moi.

(She goes R. behind the couch and exits to the wine cellar.)

VANCE. *(Gets up and starts pacing a little.)* Do you think she knows what's going on?

CONNIE. I doubt it. I mean she hasn't been here for nearly five years.

VANCE. Well somebody's got to know.

CONNIE. You said it before, Clifton seems to be the key.

VANCE. You're right, but can we persuade him to cooperate?

CONNIE. Clifton—cooperate?

VANCE. Why not? Everyone has a price.

CONNIE. Not Clifton. I think you'd have a better chance persuading Imelda Marcos to wear flip-flops!

VANCE. You're right. Maybe Mrs. Clifton is the weak link. *(Enter DAVIS from the kitchen.)* Ah Davis, we were just talking about Mrs. Clifton, do you suppose you could remain conscious long enough to interrogate her?

DAVIS. Ah yes. Sorry about that. I don't know what happened.

CONNIE. I think maybe you're allergic to doors.

VANCE. Listen, Mrs. Clifton will be in here in a minute. I'd like you to question her, very subtly of course, and try to find out what she knows about this Bimbo Corporation and who runs it.

DAVIS. Leave it to me. Subtle is my middle name. Let me just insure you that she'll never know what secrets she's repealing.

VANCE. Right, we'll leave you to it then. *(To CONNIE.)* Shall we?

(They exit U.R.)

DAVIS. I'll just get cleaned up a little and I'll be right out.

(DAVIS exits to the powder room.
Enter CLIFTON from the apartment. He is all disheveled and straightening his clothing. Enter RENEE from the wine cellar with a bottle of wine in her hand.)

RENEE. Clifton. My beautiful butler.

(She advances on him.)

CLIFTON. *(Backs away from her.)* Miss Renee, you must understand there have been some changes around here. *(Sees the bottle in her hand.)* Is that a Philip Togni cabernet?

RENEE. Mais oui.

CLIFTON. You do know, don't you, that that is a two-hundred-dollar bottle of wine?

RENEE. Two hundred dollars for this little bottle of wine. There would have to be an orgasm in every glass for it to be worth that much, *(She advances sexily again.)* and who knows, maybe there is. Anyway, we are rich n'est-ce-pas?

CLIFTON. Well, not yet.

RENEE. Oh, what has happened with the paintings?

(DAVIS opens the door of the powder room, stops and listens.)

CLIFTON. Oh, they're all sold alright, but I don't have the final accounting from Sotheby's yet, so for the moment everything is in limbo.

(DAVIS takes out a notebook and pencil and carefully and deliberately writes in it.
Enter AGNES from U.R. She again has the suspicious looking lump

under her blouse. She heads for the kitchen.)

CLIFTON. *(Stops her.)* Agnes, I don't think it's a good idea for you to go in there.

AGNES. Grow my hair? I don't want to.

CLIFTON. *(Switches on her hearing aid.)* I don't want Oscar in the kitchen.

AGNES. And why not?

CLIFTON. He'll upset Mrs. Clifton again.

AGNES. Oh, alright, I'll take him back upstairs.

(She exits U.L. looking over her shoulder to make sure CLIFTON isn't watching, then she turns off the hearing aid.)

RENEE. So Oscar still has the run of the place?

(DAVIS reacts, writes in his notebook, then exits to the powder room, closing the door.)

CLIFTON. I'm afraid so.

RENEE. Now my beautiful butler, we are alone, we shall take this wine, and you shall come with me.

(She crosses L. sexily and has him backed up against the bar. She kisses him passionately. He protests feebly. Enter SUSIE from the kitchen pushing a large trolley with serving dishes, a large wooden bowl containing salad and a silver platter with sandwiches on its upper level. A large table cloth hangs down so the lower level cannot be seen. She sees RENEE and very deliberately lines up the trolley, then pushes it against RENEE's back. RENEE's legs go forward, she buckles at the knees and falls backwards in a sitting position on top of the sandwiches.)

SUSIE. *(Smiles.)* Oh dear, I'm so sorry.

RENEE. *(Struggles up.)* O-o-o-h. My skirt, what a mess.

CLIFTON. *(Looks at SUSIE.)* Susie!

SUSIE. I said I was sorry.

RENEE. *(Running her fingers up and down CLIFTON's arm.)* I shall go and change in my lonely, lonely room and then I think I shall take a little nap in my lonely, lonely bed.

(RENEE heads U.L.)

SUSIE. I'll bet the only reason her bed is ever lonely is because she's always in someone else's.

RENEE. *(Turns by the L.C. pillar, strikes a sexy pose and blows a kiss to CLIFTON.)* Ooh-la-la!

(RENEE exits U.R.)

CLIFTON. I suppose I should thank you again.

SUSIE. That's O.K. I quite enjoyed that one. *(She picks up the platter.)* I'd better redo the sandwiches, come on *(Now mimicking Renee's French accent.)* my great big beautiful butler.

(She laughs and exits to the kitchen. CLIFTON, who is holding the kitchen door open for SUSIE, is about to follow her but "JOSEPHINE's" arm [SEE AUTHOR'S NOTE] reaches out from the apartment door and pulls him inside. The door slides silently shut.

Enter DAVIS from the powder room, frantically dialing his cell phone.)

DAVIS. Hello Vance. I've got it all, all the information you needed. *(Takes out his notebook and reads.)* Everything's in Bimbo, and Oscar runs the place! *(He goes U.L. to listen by the kitchen door, realizes he is too close to it, and leaps backwards.)* No, I haven't interviewed Mrs. Clifton yet, my information comes from extremely continental sources. Alright, I'm right on it. *(Enter SUSIE from the kitchen carrying the sandwich platter which she replaces on the trolley.)* Here she is now.

(He quickly removes the phone from his ear and tries to hide it from SUSIE by dropping it into the salad bowl.)

SUSIE. Mr. Davis, you haven't seen Clifton, have you?

DAVIS. I'm afraid not, madam.

SUSIE. That's funny, he was here a minute ago. *(She looks at the apartment door.)* No he couldn't, it's only been ten minutes.

DAVIS. If you have a moment madam, I would like to talk to you about a matter of the utmost continence.

SUSIE. I know you didn't mean that, so I'll just ignore it. Would you like to sit down? It might be safer.

DAVIS. Thank you.

(He sits on the couch L. side; SUSIE sits in the chair.)

SUSIE. That's better. Now what can I do for you?

DAVIS. *(Trying to be casual.)* Well, madam, I just happened, quite by accident—

SUSIE. You're kidding me.

DAVIS. What?

SUSIE. Never mind.

DAVIS. I just happened to come across a report about a company known as The Bimbo Corporation, and I wondered if you'd ever heard of it?

SUSIE. That's very interesting Mr. Davis. What did the report say?

DAVIS. Well, it appears that this Bimbo Corporation acquired all sorts of assets in rather strange circumstances.

SUSIE. Fascinating. What sort of circumstances?

DAVIS. Well, no one seems to know.

SUSIE. I see. What sort of assets?

DAVIS. Well, you know, yachts, cars, artwork.

SUSIE. Oh. I see.

DAVIS. You do?

SUSIE. Yes

DAVIS. What ?

SUSIE. What what?

DAVIS. What do you see?

SUSIE. What do you mean, what do I see?

DAVIS. You said "I see."

SUSIE. Yes.

DAVIS. Well, what is it you see?

SUSIE. What you said.

DAVIS. What?

SUSIE. What you said.

DAVIS. What did I say?

SUSIE. You don't know what you said?

DAVIS. Yes, I know what I said.

SUSIE. Well?

DAVIS. Well what?

SUSIE. Well, what you said.

DAVIS. I didn't say well.

SUSIE. No, you said what.

DAVIS. What what?

SUSIE. What you said.

DAVIS. Didn't we just do that?

SUSIE. Do what?

DAVIS. You know, what you said.

SUSIE. Yes.

DAVIS. Yes what?

SUSIE. Yes, we just did that.

DAVIS. Oh, I see.

SUSIE. There you see, you said it.

DAVIS. Said what?

SUSIE. You said, "I see." What do you see?

DAVIS. What?

SUSIE. Never mind.

DAVIS. *(Almost to himself.)* Maybe that's a bit too subtle.

(DAVIS gets up and starts to move around.)

SUSIE. What?

DAVIS. What what?

SUSIE. I don't think we should go down that road again.

DAVIS. I'm going to try a more direct approach.

SUSIE. Approach to what? *(Quickly realizes what she has said.)* No—forget I said that.

DAVIS. Mrs. Clifton, I'm going to ask you a very pacific question.

SUSIE. Pacific?

DAVIS. What can you tell me about Oscar?

SUSIE. What would you like to know?

DAVIS. Ah-ha! You know about him then?

SUSIE. Unfortunately, yes.

DAVIS. *(Writing in his notebook.)* I gather then that you don't like him.

SUSIE. I most certainly do not.

DAVIS. May I ask why?

SUSIE. Well, he's a rat.

DAVIS. Really?

SUSIE. A dirty stinking rat.

DAVIS. Those are rather strong words, Mrs. Clifton.

SUSIE. I don't think so.

DAVIS. I see, and just what has he ever done to you to make you feel that way?

SUSIE. Well, he's never done anything to me. I just don't want him around that's all. I just want Agnes to keep him away from me.

DAVIS. Why Agnes?

SUSIE. Well, she seems to be the only one able to control him.

DAVIS. *(Writing again.)* So, Agnes controls him. Very interesting. *(Davis's phone rings in the salad bowl. At this point, DAVIS, who has been pacing a little, is now just to the L. of Susie's chair and therefore between her and the trolley which is just above the D.L. bar. He reaches behind his back to get the phone, which he finds. He places it to his ear but a large leaf of lettuce comes with it. Watched by SUSIE, he stuffs the lettuce in his mouth and eats it. Now holding the phone very gingerly between his thumb and forefinger, he clicks it on.)* Hello, yes Mr. Vance, I'm in the wine room. Yes, *(Turns away from SUSIE.)* Yes, I've completed my interpretation of Mrs. Clifton.

SUSIE. *(Gets up.)* Look, I've got things to do in the kitchen. Excuse me.

(SUSIE exits to the kitchen.)

DAVIS. *(Still on the phone.)* I have one or two details to check on and I'll get right back to you. *(He's about to put the phone back in his pocket, when he realizes it is covered with salad dressing. He pauses and looks at it. Enter AGNES from U.L. In her left hand she is carrying a vacuum cleaner with the cord carelessly looped, dragging behind her. Under her right arm she carries a long handled mop, mop end forward. Davis sees her and hastily drops the phone back in the salad bowl. He comes U. to meet AGNES at the C. steps.)* Miss Agnes, may I have a word with you please? *(AGNES, her hearing aid clearly switched off, continues right past him on her way to the kitchen. DAVIS turns and follows a half step behind her and shouts.)* AGNES!

(DAVIS gets a loop of the vacuum cord caught around his feet and goes down. He struggles up as AGNES, brought to a halt by the cord, turns. The mop swings around and hits DAVIS in the crotch. With a groan he goes down again. AGNES just shrugs and continues on to the kitchen. DAVIS struggles to his feet as SUSIE screams in the kitchen. DAVIS creeps to the kitchen door to listen as SUSIE comes out of the door on the dead run. She flattens DAVIS behind it and he goes down again. SUSIE continues R. and stands on the couch. This time DAVIS stays down as MARJORIE enters from U.R. and comes D.

During the following conversation DAVIS recovers consciousness, sees SUSIE and MARJORIE talking, hides behind the trolley which is still just above the bar, takes out a pencil and notebook, and then hiding from them, he climbs on the lower level of the trolley. He is now concealed from view by the tablecloth. As the conversation continues, the trolley, propelled by the unseen DAVIS, moves ever so slowly R. towards the chair.)

MARJORIE. Hello.

SUSIE. *(Still standing on the couch.)* Hello.

MARJORIE. I don't believe we've met. I'm Marjorie Merivale.

SUSIE. Oh, you're the cars. Hi, I'm Susie.

MARJORIE. Hi. If you don't mind my asking, why are you standing on the couch?

SUSIE. *(Gets down and sits on the couch R. end.)* I'm sorry, but it's Oscar.

MARJORIE. He's still here?

SUSIE. Oh yes.

MARJORIE. Oh boy!

SUSIE. "Oh boy" is right, you know there's absolutely no way I'm ever going to get used to him being here.

MARJORIE. I know exactly what you mean. I could never stand him either. Tell me Susie, what do you do around here?

SUSIE. I'm Clifton's—er— wait a minute—do you mind if I ask you a question?

MARJORIE. I suppose not.

(MARJORIE sits on the chair.)

SUSIE. Did I see you kissing Clifton a bit earlier?

MARJORIE. You saw us?

SUSIE. Yes.

MARJORIE. So?

SUSIE. Well, I take it then that you and Clifton, are—er—

MARJORIE. Definitely.

SUSIE. Right, then I'm the maid.

MARJORIE. Well now Susie, if you're the maid, why did Miss Olden call you Mrs. Clifton?

SUSIE. Ah—yes—well, you see she thinks I am Mrs. Clifton.

MARJORIE. Why would she think that?

SUSIE. Well, because— *(Her eyes light up.)* I'm married to Clifton's brother. That's why I'm Mrs. Clifton.

MARJORIE. I didn't know Clifton had a brother.

SUSIE. Oh yes. He's had one for years.

MARJORIE. And you work here as the maid?

SUSIE. Yes. That's right.

MARJORIE. And your husband?

SUSIE. Yes?

MARJORIE. Is he here?

SUSIE. Well sometimes, but you won't see him, he keeps a very low profile.

MARJORIE. I see, do you know where Clifton is?

SUSIE. *(Looks at the apartment.)* I'm not absolutely sure. He just kind of disappeared.

MARJORIE. He told me he'd moved into the Rose Room, but there's nothing there, none of his clothes, nothing. *(She gets up and heads L. towards the apartment.)* I thought he said he'd moved out of his apartment, but maybe I misunderstood.

SUSIE. *(Gets up and follows her L.)* I wouldn't go in there if I were you.

MARJORIE. Oh, and why not?

(The trolley now follows them slowly L.)

SUSIE. Well—er—er. Oscar's in there.

(DAVIS's head appears briefly as he reacts to this information.)

MARJORIE. Oh, in that case you're absolutely right. I'm not going in there.

SUSIE. If you like, I could try to find Clifton for you.

MARJORIE. Thank you.

SUSIE. As a matter of fact there are a couple of things I'd like to discuss with him myself.

(SUSIE and MARJORIE exit to the kitchen.
Enter VANCE from U.R. As he comes D. he is dialing on his cell phone. DAVIS's phone in the salad bowl rings. His arm appears as he reaches over the top and grabs the phone.)

VANCE. *(Pacing above the couch.)* Hello, Davis? Where the devil are you and what's all this about Oscar running The Bimbo Corporation? Who is Oscar?

DAVIS. *(Crawls out from the trolley on its L. side and, facing L., talks into his phone.)* As a result of intensive invigorations, I have it on good austerity that Oscar runs The Bimbo Corporation.

VANCE. *(Now sees DAVIS and clicks off his phone.)* What?

DAVIS. *(Still facing D.L.)* Hello, hello.

VANCE. *(Raises his eyes heavenward.)* Hello–o–o!

DAVIS. *(Sees VANCE.)* Oh!

(DAVIS puts his phone down on the trolley.)

VANCE. Start again.

DAVIS. Oscar is the key. He runs everything, and furthermore he is controlled by Agnes.

VANCE. The housekeeper?

DAVIS. Precisely.

VANCE. Alright then, just who is this Oscar, and more importantly, where is Oscar?

DAVIS. Exactly who he is, I'm not sure yet, but there would appear to be a strong livelyhood that he is Clifton's brother.

VANCE. Clifton has a brother here?

DAVIS. Oh yes.

VANCE. Why haven't we met him?

DAVIS. He keeps a very low profile.

VANCE. Well, you're the detective. Find him.

(Enter JOSEPHINE from the apartment. She appears to be wrapped in a sheet.)

JOSEPHINE. Oh, I say I'm frightfully sorry. I hope I'm not disturbing you. I didn't know anyone was here. Please excuse the way I'm dressed. I'm just going to get some champagne.

(She giggles and exits to the wine cellar.)

DAVIS. *(Watches her go then rushes L. to the apartment door to listen.)* Perfect.

VANCE. What's perfect?

DAVIS. Sh! Oscar is in there.

VANCE. What?

DAVIS. Oscar, he's in Clifton's apartment?

VANCE. Let's go talk to him.

DAVIS. Wait a minute. You said yourself we need a more subtle approach. Let's do this, call me on your phone and we'll leave the line open, so you can hear every word while I talk to him.

VANCE. You know that's not a bad idea. *(He dials.)* You finally might have something right.

(Davis's phone, still on the trolley, rings. DAVIS picks it up and clicks it on. It is still covered with salad dressing and bits of lettuce as he handles it gingerly with thumb and forefinger.)

DAVIS. I'll just go and wash this off, you wait outside.

(DAVIS crosses R. to the powder room.)

VANCE. Right.

(VANCE heads U.S.)

DAVIS. *(Turns from the powder room door.)* Remember now, I need you to keep the secret of this method of overhearing other peoples' confirmations in the strictest confluence.

(He exits to the powder room, VANCE exits to the front door.
Enter SUSIE from the kitchen with a covered dish, which she places on the trolley, then wheels it over to just above the chair. CLIFTON staggers out of the apartment. He is clearly trying to escape and looks furtively around before stepping into the room. His vest and tie are in his hand, his shirt unbuttoned and hanging outside his pants, which he is fastening as he enters.)

SUSIE. *(Laughs.)* How's your little English rose?

CLIFTON. *(Tucking in his shirt and getting dressed.)* Oh dear, things are getting out of hand.

SUSIE. You're telling me!

CLIFTON. *(Crosses R. to her, above the trolley.)* Miss Legere, please believe me when I tell you that I never intended to get into this sort of mess. If you would please help me get through the day, I really would be most appreciative.

SUSIE. Oh I wouldn't miss this for the world, and I'm trying to help you, I really am. As a matter of fact I've just had a most interesting conversation with—er—the American one.

CLIFTON. Miss Merivale.

SUSIE. The one with the cars whose cleavage looks like silicone valley. She's looking for you.

CLIFTON. Yes, I thought she might be.

SUSIE. May I give you some advice?

CLIFTON. What?

(Enter MARJORIE from the kitchen.)

SUSIE. *(Giggles.)* You'd better start taking vitamins.

(SUSIE exits to the kitchen.)

MARJORIE. *(Waits until SUSIE has gone then flings herself at CLIFTON.)* Clifton—alone at last!

(She embraces him in a long passionate kiss.)

CLIFTON. *(Eventually.)* Oh Marjorie!

(He looks nervously around.)

MARJORIE. You're looking a little frazzled Clifton, is

everything alright?

CLIFTON. Well, yes and no.

MARJORIE. Why don't you come and sit down and relax. I want to talk to you about our future.

(They hold hands and go down to the couch.)

CLIFTON. Well maybe we should talk about that a little bit.

(They sit.)

MARJORIE. You know it's strange isn't it?

CLIFTON. What is?

MARJORIE. Well, I lived with Billy for almost three years and I suppose I was in love with him, and for nearly all that time you were just the butler. I mean I never thought of you as—well—you know.

CLIFTON. You mean when you looked at me the words sensual and erotic barbarian never crossed your mind.

MARJORIE. *(Laughs.)* Well, no.

CLIFTON. Be that as it may, I need to talk to you about Miss Josephine.

MARJORIE. Who?

CLIFTON. The—er—the one who followed you.

MARJORIE. Oh the English fruit cake. I heard about her.

CLIFTON. Hardly a fruit cake, my dear. You probably don't know this, but she has a doctorate in psychology.

MARJORIE. Oh yeah? I'm sure that was probably what attracted Billy, her P.H. double D. Anyway, what about her?

CLIFTON. Well, after you left, she kind of moved in.

MARJORIE. So? I always knew Billy and I weren't forever. He just wasn't that sort of man.

CLIFTON. No, you don't understand, you see, when I said she moved in, I didn't mean she moved right in with Mr. Olden, which of course she did, I meant she moved right in with—

MARJORIE. Talking of moving in, why did you tell me you'd moved to the Rose Room?

CLIFTON. Ah, well, yes, you see that's what I'm trying to tell you. *(He looks nervously around clearly wondering where JOSEPHINE could be.)* You see Miss Josephine—oh dear.

MARJORIE. Clifton, what are you so nervous about?

(She leans over and kisses him lightly.
Enter SUSIE from the kitchen.)

SUSIE. Oh excuse me.

MARJORIE. *(Gets up.)* That's alright, it's just that we have a little catching up to do. Clifton and I were just going to his apartment.

CLIFTON. We were?

MARJORIE. Susie, perhaps you would be good enough to put a nice bottle of champagne on ice for us for later. I have a feeling we're going to need it. *(She gives CLIFTON a peck on the lips.)* Give me five minutes to slip into something more comfortable, then come and get me you sensual erotic barbarian!

(She crosses L. and exits to the apartment.)

SUSIE. Sensual, erotic barbarian?

CLIFTON. Let it go.

SUSIE. You know, you hired me to protect you from "ooh-la-la," but I'm just beginning to get the big picture.

CLIFTON. Please believe me, I'm not used to this sort of thing. My relationship with Miss Josephine and Miss Marjorie just kind of got out of hand. I've not had very much experience in my life saying no to women. In fact, if the truth be told, I've not had very much experience with women.

SUSIE. Well, you could have fooled me.

CLIFTON. What are we going to do?

SUSIE. We?

CLIFTON. Please, there's a great deal at stake.

SUSIE. O.K. Where's your little English rose?

CLIFTON. She said she was going to the wine cellar to get some champagne.

SUSIE. Right, here we go then. Take your vitamins and get down to the wine cellar and keep her quiet. I'll figure out a way to distract silicone valley.

CLIFTON. Thank you, Susie.

SUSIE. You're welcome. *(She gives him a little kiss on the cheek then giggles.)* You sensual erotic barbarian!

(She exits to the kitchen giggling. CLIFTON exits to the wine cellar. Enter DAVIS from the powder room. He has his phone to his ear.)

DAVIS. Mr. Vance, can you hear me? O.K. good, stand by. Now I'm going to confront Oscar. Here we go then.

(He creeps up to the apartment door and enters furtively. There is a scream from MARJORIE, followed by a dull thud followed by an agonizing groan from DAVIS. DAVIS enters from the apartment holding his crotch. He is followed by MARJORIE holding a broom. DAVIS falls to his knees. MARJORIE whacks him on the backside. He gets up and staggers R. He still has his cell phone.)

MARJORIE. You pervert.

DAVIS. Really madam, I—

MARJORIE. Just who the hell are you anyway?

DAVIS. *(Backing away R. from MARJORIE brandishing the broom.)* Please madam, I shall be forced to defend myself.

MARJORIE. You revolting little maggot. What do you think you were doing?

(At this point she has him backed off immediately to the L. of the chair He quickly drops his cell phone into the salad bowl so his hands are free to strike his karate pose.)

DAVIS. Hi-ya!

(He takes a half step back, falls backwards over the arm of the chair and ends up unconscious on the floor.
Enter CONNIE from U.R. as VANCE, his cell phone to his ear, rushes in the front door. They all look at DAVIS.)

VANCE. What happened? There was this dreadful noise.
CONNIE. Good grief, he's unconscious again.

(CONNIE and VANCE move to sit on the couch.)

MARJORIE. Are you just going to leave him there?
CONNIE. We've figured out the floor is the safest place for him.
MARJORIE. Who is he anyway?
CONNIE. He's another one of Mr. Vance's brilliant ideas.
VANCE. Exactly who he is—is not important.
MARJORIE. Well he came creeping into Clifton's apartment just as I was about to get undressed, he never knocked or anything.
CONNIE. Yes, he tends to do that.

(The door to the wine cellar slides open and CLIFTON looks into the room. He has a bottle of champagne in his hand. He sees MARJORIE and turns to the unseen "JOSEPHINE.")

CLIFTON. I have a better idea. Let's have our champagne in the wine cellar. We can share that couch. I'll get some food. Won't be a minute.

(Two hands ruffle his hair and stroke his face, before he hurriedly

pushes "JOSEPHINE" away and closes the door. [SEE AUTHOR'S NOTE])

MARJORIE. What do you mean share that couch? Who's that?
CLIFTON. No, no, I said I can't bear that grouch.
MARJORIE. Grouch, what grouch, who are you getting food for?
CLIFTON. Er—er—Oscar. Yes, he's hungry.
MARJORIE. Oh, I see.
VANCE. Oscar is in the wine cellar?
CLIFTON. Definitely.
MARJORIE. Well, I see you've got the champagne. *(She takes CLIFTON by the arm and leads him L. She stops by the apartment door.)* Put it on ice, lover boy, I'll see you in a minute.

(She gives him a quick kiss and exits to the apartment.)

CLIFTON. Oh dear!

(CLIFTON exits to the kitchen.)

DAVIS. *(Groans and staggers to his feet.)* What happened?
CONNIE. Why do you always ask us that?
VANCE. Now, are you ready to interview Oscar?
CONNIE. Who's Oscar?
VANCE. We think he's the key to The Bimbo Corporation.
CONNIE. Oscar who?
DAVIS. Clifton's brother.
CONNIE. I didn't know Clifton had a brother.
VANCE. I'll explain later. *(To DAVIS.)* Right now you need to get moving because Oscar is in the wine cellar.
DAVIS. How did he get down there?
VANCE. How he got there doesn't matter. You need to talk to him. Now remember, be subtle, you need to coax the information out

of him.

DAVIS. I've already told you, subtle is my middle name. He'll never know he's being invigorated.

(He exits to the wine cellar, moving through the door in a furtive manner.
Enter AGNES from the kitchen.)

VANCE. Ah Agnes, we'd like a word with you please. *(AGNES, her hearing aid switched off, ignores this. VANCE crosses quietly and places himself squarely in front of her.)* Agnes, we'd like to talk to you.

AGNES. Chalk my cue? I don't play pool.

VANCE. *(Indicates the couch, takes her by the elbow and guides her R.)* Please sit down.

(They all sit, VANCE in the chair, CONNIE couch R. side, AGNES couch L. side.)

CONNIE. You'd better speak up, you know she's deaf.

VANCE. *(Loud, slow and deliberate.)* We'd like to talk to you about Oscar.

AGNES. I can't hear you, and anyway I don't want to talk about Oscar.

CONNIE. *(Points to AGNES's hearing aid.)* Can we switch this on?

AGNES. *(Switches it on.)* Alright, but the batteries are weak and I might not hear you.

CONNIE. Especially if you don't want to.

AGNES. I heard that.

CONNIE. Good. Now hear this. We know about Oscar.

AGNES. What do you mean?

VANCE. Mr. Davis said you were able to control Oscar. Is that true?

AGNES. What if it is?

VANCE. Then we'd like to meet him.

AGNES. You would?

VANCE. Yes, we're very anxious to get to know him.

AGNES. *(Suspicious.)* Why?

(VANCE looks to CONNIE for help.)

CONNIE. Well, er—he's part of Clifton's family and this household, and we'd like to, you know—er—sit down and chew the fat a little bit.

AGNES. Oh he'd like that.

VANCE. Good.

AGNES. I'll go and find him if you like.

VANCE. Well, he's in the wine cellar with Mr. Davis right now.

AGNES. No he's not.

CONNIE. I beg your pardon?

AGNES. He's not allowed in the wine cellar.

CONNIE. Why not?

AGNES. Well, he gets in all the bottles.

CONNIE. Oh, I see.

AGNES. It's so nice to find someone who likes Oscar. I think he'd enjoy meeting you.

CONNIE. I shall forward to meeting him.

AGNES. I think I know where he is, I'll go and get him if you like.

VANCE. Well thank you, Agnes. I'll tell you what, why don't we come with you. *(AGNES switches off and heads U.R. followed by CONNIE and VANCE.)* Oscar gets into the bottles. He's got a drinking problem then. Maybe we can use that to our advantage.

(Exeunt U.R.

Enter CLIFTON from the kitchen followed by SUSIE, carrying the champagne in an ice bucket, which she puts on the bar.)

CLIFTON. I've got a feeling something's going to go wrong. I can't even remember which one the champagne is for.

SUSIE. *(Sits on one of the bar stools.)* Well, well, you have got yourself into a pickle haven't you.

CLIFTON. Oh please!

SUSIE. How in heavens name did you manage to have an affair with English and Silicone Valley at the same time?

CLIFTON. Well, you see, they never really were at the same time. After Miss Marjorie moved out, we kept in touch because I was working on selling the cars, and we sort of became—er—romantically involved.

SUSIE. I presume that was after you'd got you hands on the money?

CLIFTON. Yes, but—oh you're not suggesting—

SUSIE. No, not at all. What about English?

CLIFTON. Well after she broke up with Mr. Olden, about six months ago, and we were working on getting the yacht moved we—er—well—er—

SUSIE. Became romantically involved?

CLIFTON. Exactly.

SUSIE. I'm curious. Before or after the yacht was sold?

CLIFTON. Just about that time I guess. Oh dear! It can't be the money. *(He is now pacing a little to SUSIE's R.)* I promised all of them to share the money equally.

SUSIE. You mean you get half of the proceeds from the yacht and the cars?

CLIFTON. And the paintings. Don't forget the paintings.

SUSIE. But that's—

CLIFTON. A little over thirty million dollars, miss.

SUSIE. Wow!

CLIFTON. Wow is right.

SUSIE. You mean you figured out they would contest the will?

CLIFTON. Exactly.

SUSIE. *(She pauses.)* Then you own The Bimbo Corporation?

CLIFTON. I'm afraid so.

SUSIE. And you promised each of these three bimbos—"ladies" half of their portion?

CLIFTON. Yes.

SUSIE. I see. Tell me Clifton, just how did this Bimbo Corporation come to own the paintings, the cars and the yacht?

CLIFTON. Ah, well now, that's a good question.

SUSIE. I know. That's why I asked it.

CLIFTON. Well, in a nutshell, I was able to persuade Mr. Olden to sign the necessary papers.

SUSIE. Oh well, that's all right then. Wait a minute, *(She pauses.)* did he know what he was doing?

CLIFTON. Well now, that's another good question, miss. *(SUSIE just looks at him.)* Look, he wrote in his will that he wanted them to have those things.

SUSIE. You didn't answer my question.

CLIFTON. I know, probably because I'm honestly not sure of the answer.

SUSIE. *(Pauses.)* You need help.

CLIFTON. I know.

SUSIE. I meant with English and Silicone Valley.

CLIFTON. That's what I meant too. What do you think we should do?

SUSIE. I don't know, but what I do know is that there's no way to keep this going with both of them in the same house at the same time.

CLIFTON. I know. Anyway, I don't think I really want to keep it going.

SUSIE. Now that's the first sensible thing you've said today.

Alright, let me think—hmm—Maybe we should just let them meet each other.

CLIFTON. Somehow I don't think that's going to work, and anyway it's just about the worst idea since Hitler's dad winked at his wife and said "Let's go upstairs."

(He hears voices in the wine cellar and moves R. to center stage.
Enter DAVIS from the wine cellar followed by JOSEPHINE still wearing her sheet. She is holding a wine bottle by the neck and threatening to hit DAVIS with it. He backs away L. almost to the kitchen door.)

JO. Clifton, thank goodness you're here. I caught this bounder creeping around in the wine cellar.

DAVIS. I was not creeping around.

JO. Oh, and what would you call it?

SUSIE. Please don't answer that.

JO. We have a word in England for weirdos like you.

DAVIS. I can assure you miss, that my inventions were highly honorable, and that I merely perspired to inverberate the other personage responsible for embezzling certain artichokes from this constabulary.

(They all look blankly at each other.)

SUSIE. Don't anyone ask. We'll be here all night.

JO. *(Comes L. to CLIFTON.)* Well I see the maid's got the champagne nice and cold, and, cozy as it was in the wine cellar, I think it's about time we—you know!

(She nods sexily towards the apartment.)

CLIFTON. Oh dear!

(CLIFTON moves hesitantly U.L. towards the apartment and mouths the word "help" to SUSIE as JOSEPHINE follows behind him. SUSIE, very deliberately, sticks out her foot causing JOSEPHINE to trip and fall into DAVIS. Their heads hit with a thump, they stagger back holding their heads, then both crumple unconscious to the floor.)

SUSIE. Oops!

CLIFTON. I asked for a little help, not Armageddon.

SUSIE. Sorry! It was all I could think of. Now what?

CLIFTON. Well, you saved the day for the moment.

SUSIE. Do you think they're hurt?

CLIFTON. *(Looks at DAVIS.)* Well, he's used to it, but perhaps we should give Miss Josephine some assistance.

(SUSIE shrieks and points to the apartment door as it starts to slide open. CLIFTON hurls himself at it and gets it shut.)

CLIFTON. Just a minute, my love, it seems to be stuck. *(He turns to SUSIE.)* Can you get her out of the way? *(SUSIE tries to lift JOSEPHINE, but she can't manage the weight on her own. She struggles and, with CLIFTON holding the door with one hand and helping SUSIE with the other, they manage to get her on the lower level of the trolley. Her head and torso are covered, but her lower legs and feet are sticking out at one end.)* Good, now get her out of sight. *(SUSIE turns the trolley to try to maneuver it into the kitchen, but DAVIS is in the way. She looks around, the only other door is the powder room. She heads for it as CLIFTON calls out.)* Just a minute, my love, I'll get it fixed, it seems to be off the track. *(SUSIE opens the powder room door and pushes the trolley inside. [SEE AUTHOR'S NOTES.] There is a momentary pause then a scream from SUSIE who immediately reappears with the trolley.)* What's wrong?

SUSIE. Oscar's in there.

CLIFTON. Oh Lord! I'll have to sacrifice myself. Give me the champagne *quickly.*

SUSIE. *(Rushes over to the bar, picks up the champagne and ice bucket, then comes U.S. to CLIFTON.)* Listen, I've got an idea. Give me five minutes then get her out of there and into this room.

CLIFTON. *(Takes the champagne bottle, leaving SUSIE holding the ice bucket)* O.K. Please hurry. *(Turns to the door.)* I think I've got it fixed, my little California angel. I've got the champagne, get ready, here comes your lean mean butlering machine.

(With a last wistful look at SUSIE, who raises her eyes heavenward, he exits to the apartment and slides the door shut.
SUSIE steps over DAVIS and exits to the kitchen, carrying the ice bucket. DAVIS groans and starts to stand up holding his head. SUSIE, now minus the ice bucket, rushes out of the kitchen and heads for the front door, and exits. The kitchen door hits DAVIS again and down he goes.
Enter AGNES, CONNIE and VANCE from U.R.)

AGNES. I'm sorry, I have no idea where Oscar has got to. He'll come into the kitchen when he's hungry. I'll wait for him there.

(Totally ignoring the prone figure of DAVIS, she steps over him and exits to the kitchen. DAVIS groans and sits up.)

CONNIE. What happened?

DAVIS. It's that door again.

VANCE. Why don't you just stay in the middle of the room?

CONNIE. *(Sits on the couch, L. side.)* Maybe you should sit down.

DAVIS. Thank you, I'll be alright in a minute.

(DAVIS sits in the chair.)

CONNIE. Can I get you anything?

DAVIS. Thank you. I'm fine. *(He pauses and turns to VANCE.)* How would I ever leave the room?

VANCE. What?

CONNIE. Please don't answer that.

VANCE. This is ridiculous.

CONNIE. What is?

VANCE. *(Pacing a little behind the couch.)* Think about it. It's stupid. Here we are, wandering around this mansion, following a housekeeper who's ten years older than Moses, she's as deaf as a post and moves about as fast as one, and why are we doing this? Because Mr. "I can't stay conscious for more than five minutes" Davis here says a guy called Oscar, that no one has ever seen, has embezzled everything in sight, and who I'm not sure exists at all.

DAVIS. I can assure you, Mr. Vance, that Oscar is very real. That fact has been infirmed to me both by Mrs. Clifton and er—Miss—er—the redhead.

CONNIE. Miss Sykes.

DAVIS. Miss Sykes, who has known him for years.

VANCE. *(Sits on the couch R. side.)* Well maybe you're right. I just don't see how Agnes could be in control of anything or anyone. I mean you've seen her.

DAVIS. Are you doubting the accuracy of my information?

CONNIE. Can you believe it? He got that right. Mr. Davis, we're just suggesting that you may be mistaken, even perhaps a little confused, after all, you did take a nasty blow to your head earlier.

DAVIS. I can assure you that I am highly cognizant of everything that's going on around here. *(Davis's cell phone in the salad bowl rings. He strides purposefully L. and picks up the phone on the bar.)* Hello, hello. *(The phone on the trolley continues to ring.)* Hello. *(The phone on the trolley rings again. He realizes what is wrong, smiles at*

CONNIE and VANCE, and then moves the phone to his other ear.) Hello. *(The phone on the trolley rings again. He finally figures it out, replaces the phone on the bar and crosses R. to the trolley, still outside the powder room door.)* Yes, nothing escapes my attention, my eyes are everywhere. *(He gropes around in the salad bowl and finally finds the phone, covered with salad, which gets all over him. While doing this, he looks directly at "JOSEPHINE's" feet, but they fail to register.)* Hello, yes, I see, very interesting—thank you. *(He clicks off the phone and comes back up to the chair while eating various pieces of salad stuck to the phone.)* As I was saying, nothing is beyond reach of the William Davis Agency.

(He pauses.)

VANCE. What?

DAVIS. We've located one of the cars.

VANCE. And?

DAVIS. A "J" model Duesenberg sold privately to a Mr. William Worthington of Massachusetts for one point five million dollars.

VANCE. And?

DAVIS. Sold by—

CONNIE, VANCE and DAVIS. *(Together.)* The Bimbo Corporation!

VANCE. We're no further ahead than when we started.

CONNIE. On the contrary, Mr. Vance, I'm certainly no further ahead than when we started, but you, and I do emphasize the word "you," are one million dollars behind where you started.

DAVIS. What?

CONNIE. Oh didn't he tell you? He paid a million bucks for a paint-by-numbers picture.

DAVIS. And you call me stupid!

VANCE. Let's get back to this Oscar fellow. Until we track him down, The Bimbo Corporation is the only lead we've got. It's surely not too great a feat of imagination to realize there has been a king-size embezzlement here.

DAVIS. Feet!

CONNIE. What?

DAVIS. Feet, I saw some feet.

CONNIE. What in heaven's name are you talking about?

DAVIS. Feet. I can't seem to remember where I saw the feet.

CONNIE. You're nuts. You're all nuts. How did I ever get mixed up with you two?

VANCE. I think we should make one more swing around the house for Oscar. *(They all get up.)* Davis, why don't you and Miss Olden do the main stairs, I'll do the west side, and that way, if he's up there, we can't miss him.

(VANCE exits U.L.)

CONNIE. I still think you're both nuts, but alright. Come along Mr. Davis.

(CONNIE exits U.R.)

DAVIS. *(As he follows CONNIE U.R.)* Feet, there were definitely some feet.

(Enter AGNES from the kitchen. She is clearly looking for "Oscar.")

AGNES. Oscar, Oscar. *(She crosses R. looking behind the coach etc. She notices the trolley still D.R. by the powder room door and wheels it back to the kitchen.)* Come on Oscar, I've got your favorite sandwiches, they're in the kitchen, come on Oscar.

(AGNES exits to kitchen.
Enter SUSIE from the front door, just in time to see AGNES take the trolley into the kitchen. She is now dressed in totally different

clothes, wearing a wig and glasses and very, very, pregnant! She should not easily be recognized by the audience and, if possible, not recognized at all.)

SUSIE. Clifton! *(She starts to sob.)* Oh, Clifton— *(Really howling now.)* Clifton! *(She moves R. and perches on the arm of the chair. Enter CLIFTON from the apartment, his clothes just a little awry, his vest undone. He is followed by MARJORIE, dressed as before and primping her hair a little. SUSIE hauls herself to her feet and moves L. towards them.)* Oh Clifton, how could you do this to me? And the baby due any day now. You promised to be faithful! Oh the minister was right, he warned me about you before we were married. He said a leopard doesn't change its spots.

CLIFTON. What?

MARJORIE. Clifton, who is this?

CLIFTON. I have absolutely no idea.

SUSIE. *(Howls at this.)* Ooh now you say you don't know me, how can you deny your own child?

(She pats her belly.)

MARJORIE. Clifton, what's going on here?

SUSIE. *(Crosses L. in front of CLIFTON to MARJORIE.)* Did he deceive you too? The minister told me. I should have listened. But it's too late now.

(She howls and pats her belly again.)

MARJORIE. Clifton, you'd better start talking.

CLIFTON. I haven't the remotest idea what to say.

SUSIE. Oh you knew what to say when you seduced me alright. I don't even think you would have married me if my father hadn't forced you.

CLIFTON. Your father?

SUSIE. Yes, Daddy made you do the right thing.

CLIFTON. He did?

MARJORIE. So this is how it's been has it, Clifton?

CLIFTON. No, no, you don't understand—

SUSIE. He promised me, he took his wedding vows—forsaking all others he said—O-o-o-h.

(SUSIE is sobbing and howling again.)

CLIFTON. Marjorie my dear, I can explain this, it's all a terrible misunderstanding.

SUSIE. *(Sticks her belly out and holds it.)* You call this a misunderstanding?

MARJORIE. I've heard just about enough. I'd heard rumors about little Miss English P.H. double D. but I chose to ignore them and trust you, Clifton. But this is too much.

CLIFTON. Oh dear!

MARJORIE. Oh dear? Is that all you can say? Oh dear?

CLIFTON. Yes.

MARJORIE. Well, I'm leaving. Before I get my things I would like you to write me a check for my share of the cars.

CLIFTON. Well—er—

SUSIE. O-o-h!

(SUSIE starts to howl again.)

CLIFTON. Right away.

(He goes to the bar and writes.)

SUSIE. I don't blame you, I know how irresistible he is. *(Sobbing again.)* I should have listened to the minister. He said he was no good.

MARJORIE. Now, now my dear, it'll be alright. He's all yours now, after all he did marry you.

SUSIE. Yes, but can I ever trust him again?

(SUSIE howls.)

CLIFTON. *(Stands with the check in his hand.)* Marjorie, I—

MARJORIE. *(Reaches over, takes the check out of his hand and looks at it.)* Wow! *(She looks at CLIFTON, then the check, then CLIFTON again.)* I'm outa here.

(MARJORIE exits U.R.)

SUSIE. *(Whips off her wig and glasses.)* Well, one down and one to go.

CLIFTON. That was quite a performance.

SUSIE. Listen, you don't get equity contracts unless you're good. I told you, you got yourself an actress.

CLIFTON. You were fantastic.

SUSIE. I had you fooled didn't I?

CLIFTON. Well, at first, yes.

SUSIE. What gave it away?

CLIFTON. Well, it was the "forsaking all others."

SUSIE. Yes, that was a bit overdone wasn't it.

CLIFTON. You know I'll be eternally grateful to you, but why are you doing all this for me?

SUSIE. *(Looks at him.)* Let's just say I like you, and anyway, you hired me to do a job. Well, I'd better get changed. My things are in the car. *(She heads for the front door, then turns.)* Oh, by the way, English is in the kitchen with Agnes.

(SUSIE exits through front door.)

CLIFTON. Thanks, I'll see if she's O.K.

(He heads for the kitchen.
Enter VANCE from U.L. He sees CLIFTON.)

VANCE. Ah, Mr. Clifton, just the man I'm looking for.

CLIFTON. Yes, I thought you might be.

VANCE. Why don't you and I have that little chat now, Clifton.

CLIFTON. As you wish, sir.

VANCE. *(He indicates the chair. CLIFTON sits while VANCE paces about the room.)* Now let me recap the situation for you. At some time before his death, Mr. Olden's yacht was owned and subsequently sold by The Bimbo Corporation. We have already discovered that the art collection was owned by this same company, and we have just received word that at least one of the classic cars was also owned by this Bimbo Corporation.

CLIFTON. Really, sir?

VANCE. Yes really. It appears that many valuable assets of Mr. Olden's estate mysteriously found their way into this Bimbo Corporation. *(CLIFTON looks blank.)* Now, Clifton, I'm going to ask you a question and I would advise you to think very carefully before answering. What can you tell me about this Bimbo Corporation? *(Pause. There is no response from CLIFTON.)* Well?

CLIFTON. You advised me to think carefully before answering, and I'm doing just that.

(Enter CONNIE from U.R. She is in a hurry and very agitated.)

CONNIE. Mr. Vance, Clifton. It's Davis, I need some help.

VANCE. What has he done now?

CONNIE. Well, you know that suit of armor at the foot of the main stairs.

CLIFTON. Yes, of course.

CONNIE. Well, he sort of attacked it.

CLIFTON. And?

CONNIE. I think you'd better come and see for yourself.

CLIFTON. Oh Lord! *(To VANCE.)* I'll go sir.

CONNIE. Thank you, Clifton.

(CONNIE and CLIFTON exit U.R.

Enter AGNES from the kitchen. She wheels in the trolley—now without JOSEPHINE's legs—which she leaves just above the chair. VANCE, who is standing just above the couch, ducks down out of her sight and watches.)

AGNES. Oscar? Where are you? I've got your lunch ready. Come on, you can't hide all day. It's alright, I won't let the others find you, I promise. Oscar.

(She exits U.L. looking for "Oscar." VANCE stands up, rubs his hands together in satisfaction and follows her. He exits U.L.

Enter CONNIE, DAVIS and CLIFTON from U.R. DAVIS has a huge medieval armored helmet on his head. It is on sideways. They lead him D. and sit him on the chair.)

CONNIE. Are you alright? *(Muffled sounds from within the helmet, so she lifts the visor, but all we can see is an ear.)* Are you alright?

(Muffled sounds from within the helmet.)

CLIFTON. *(Tries to pull the helmet off.)* Here let me try this. *(Louder noises from DAVIS.)* Maybe we can twist it off. Miss Constance, would you hold his shoulders please. *(She does and CLIFTON tries to turn his head; even louder noises from DAVIS.)* How in heaven's name did he manage this?

CONNIE. I'm not exactly sure, it all happened very quickly. He did one of his karate things and the whole suit of armor sort of collapsed on him.

CLIFTON. Well, if it went on, it's got to come off.

(He twists again—more yells from DAVIS.)

CONNIE. Maybe it needs lubricating.

CLIFTON. That's probably a good idea.

CONNIE. *(Picks up a bottle from the trolley.)* There's some olive oil here.

CLIFTON. O.K. Let's give it a whirl.

(He opens the visor and pours olive oil inside. There are muffled protests from within the helmet.
Enter SUSIE from the front door, now dressed in her original outfit.)

SUSIE. *(Sees DAVIS.)* Who's that?

CONNIE. It's poor Mr. Davis.

(Noise from within the helmet.)

SUSIE. *(Giggles.)* Would you like some vinegar?

CLIFTON. *(Puts the olive oil back on the trolley.)* That's not funny.

(Noises off. There is a groan from the kitchen.)

SUSIE. Oops! *(Heads for the kitchen.)* It sounds like English is back with us. *(Looks inside the kitchen door.)* Yep, she's moving. Time to go to work.

CLIFTON. What do you mean, time to go to work?

SUSIE. *(Moving D.L. towards the bar.)* I told you, one down and one to go.

(During the following conversation, SUSIE removes her bra from under her blouse. She twists and turns, wriggles and contorts. Every time CONNIE looks at her, which she does several times, she is caught frozen in a different pose, always managing to carry if off in a nonchalant manner, either by pretending to straighten her clothing or looking at her fingernails or fluffing her hair, etc.)

CONNIE. Don't you think we should do something?

SUSIE. I don't know. Maybe if we got him the rest of the suit, he'd be safer.

CLIFTON. *(Sees SUSIE wriggling.)* What are you doing?

SUSIE. You'll see.

CONNIE. Look, he can't just wear this thing for the rest of his life.

SUSIE. At least with that thing on his head he'll be safe from all the doors.

(Noises from within the helmet.)

CONNIE. Clifton, your wife doesn't seem to understand the seriousness of this situation.

CLIFTON. O.K. Let's give it one more go.

(He stands on the chair and tries to lift the helmet. It stays on. DAVIS screams as his whole body is lifted up.)

CONNIE. I think we're probably going to have to cut it off.

CLIFTON. We can't do that.

CONNIE. Why not?

CLIFTON. It's a very rare fifteenth-century piece.

SUSIE. Maybe if you put his head in the shower, warm water might expand it a little.

(Protests from within the helmet.)

CONNIE. Now that actually makes some sense. Come along Mr. Davis.

(She helps him up and, assisted by CLIFTON, walks him up the steps.)

SUSIE. I'm sure they can manage without you, Clifton.
CLIFTON. *(Turns D.S.)* Yes, but—
SUSIE. I need you here.

(She beckons to him.)

CLIFTON. Oh, O.K. You take him up, Miss Constance, I'll be along in a minute.

(CONNIE and DAVIS exit U.R.)
SUSIE, seen by the audience but not by CLIFTON, has now extracted the bra from under her jacket and is holding it behind her back. CLIFTON comes D. L. to SUSIE by the bar as JOSEPHINE, still in her sheet, enters from the kitchen. Quick as a flash, Susie drops her skirt, steps out of it, hooks her bra strap over one of CLIFTON's hands, then embraces him in a long passionate kiss.)

JO. Well, excuse me! *(SUSIE quickly separates herself from CLIFTON and retrieves her skirt, which she puts back on. CLIFTON is left standing there, holding Susie's bra and wondering how it got there.)* Clifton, what do you think you're doing?
CLIFTON. I really have absolutely no idea.
JO. You were kissing the maid.

(SUSIE giggles and holds her hands up in front of her chest.)

CLIFTON. I was?

JO. Don't play the little innocent with me. How could you do this to me?

CLIFTON. Oh Josephine, my little English Rose—

SUSIE. Little English Rose? But you said I was your little prairie flower.

CLIFTON. I did?

SUSIE. *(Turns to JOSEPHINE.)* I'm sorry if we embarrassed you. I'm sure you understand how it can be, it's just that for these past six months, we don't seem to be able to keep our hands off each other.

JO. Six months! Clifton how could you?

CLIFTON. But Josephine—

JO. Don't "but Josephine" me, you miserable, philandering two-timing cheating heap of hypocrisy.

SUSIE. Heap of hypocrisy. Oh you're good. I've got to remember that. *(All sexy now.)* Excuse us. Come on lover boy, we've finished the lunch trolley, let's take a break in our apartment.

JO. *Our* apartment. I think not. I'm going in there, I'm going to get dressed, and there is just one thing I'm going to do before I leave.

SUSIE. What's that?

JO. Collect a check for my half of the yacht.

SUSIE. He'll get it for you right away, won't you darling.

CLIFTON. Yes darling.

(JOSEPHINE stands for a moment, looks at CLIFTON, proudly shakes her head and exits to the apartment.)

SUSIE. Boy, that was almost too easy.

CLIFTON. *(Looking at the bra in his hand.)* How did that get there?

SUSIE. You don't remember?

CLIFTON. What?

SUSIE. I'm just kidding. Now let's get moving. You'd better write her that check.

CLIFTON. Oh yes, right. *(Still confused, he looks at the bra again.)* Is this yours?

SUSIE. *(Takes it from him.)* Yes, of course it's mine.

CLIFTON. *(Goes to the bar to write the check.)* Things are almost moving too fast around here.

SUSIE. Well now Clifton, it had occurred to me that it was you who were the fast mover.

CLIFTON. I tried to tell you before, I just sort of drifted into those situations.

SUSIE. Well, you're free of them now.

CLIFTON. Yes, thank you, I think.

SUSIE. Well just watch it, we don't want you drifting back anywhere do we?

CLIFTON. I suppose not. *(He pauses and looks at her.)* I guess you'll be leaving now.

SUSIE. Absolutely not. You hired me to protect you from "Ooh-la-la."

CLIFTON. Well yes, but now that Miss Josephine and Miss Marjorie have gone I thought that—well—you know, Miss Renee—

SUSIE. I don't believe this. Are you suggesting that you don't want me running interference any more?

CLIFTON. Well—er—I thought Miss Renee and I—

SUSIE. You've got to be kidding me! Anyway, we have a contract.

CLIFTON. I could fire you.

SUSIE. No you couldn't

CLIFTON. Why not?

SUSIE. It's in the contract.

CLIFTON. Well I could just tell you not to work.

SUSIE. No you couldn't.

CLIFTON. Why not?

SUSIE. It's in the contract, that would constitute a lockout. Anyway I'm not leaving you in the clutches of that predator.

CLIFTON. Oh that's a bit strong isn't it?

SUSIE. Listen, I bet more men have kissed her than bishops have kissed the Pope's ring.

CLIFTON. *(Gets up.)* I'll just take Josephine her check.

SUSIE. *(Takes the check out of his hand.)* I think perhaps I'll give it to her, and anyway you'd better go help Miss Olden with Davis, before he drowns.

CLIFTON. Oh Lord! I'd forgotten about them. You know, what we need is a big crowbar, and I think I remember seeing one in the potting shed. Tell them I'll be right back.

(CLIFTON exits through the front door.)

SUSIE. *(Goes up to the apartment door and knocks, slides it open an inch or two and calls in.)* I have your check.

("JOSEPHINE's" [SEE AUTHOR'S NOTES.] arm appears and takes the check. SUSIE exits to the kitchen.
Enter CONNIE from U.R. She is accompanied by DAVIS still wearing the helmet. He is dripping wet and clearly in physical discomfort as he is helped along by CONNIE. Enter VANCE from U.L.)

CONNIE. Mr. Vance, thank goodness you're here.

VANCE. Who or what, in heaven's name, is that?

CONNIE. It's Mr. Davis. I'm beginning to get quite worried about him.

VANCE. How did he manage that?

CONNIE. It doesn't matter how it got there. I really think we need to get it off.

VANCE. Here, sit down. *(DAVIS sits in the chair.)* Let me give it a try, this should do it.

(He twists and pulls—loud moans from DAVIS, but the helmet does not budge. Enter CLIFTON from the front door. He has a large iron crow bar in his hands.)

CLIFTON. *(Comes D.)* Let me have a go, sir, this should do it. Miss Constance would you sit on him please *(She sits on his lap.)* and Mr. Vance, perhaps you would be kind enough to hold his shoulders. *(VANCE does.)* Thank you, now—*(He inserts the crow bar under the helmet, and pushes and shoves. There is a long agonized moan from inside the helmet, but nothing moves.)* Oh dear, let's try him on the floor. *(They get him on the floor D.C.)* Miss Constance, would you sit on his chest. *(She does.)* Perhaps if you hold his feet, sir.

(VANCE holds his feet as CLIFTON inserts the crow bar. There is an enormous yell from DAVIS but this time the helmet comes off. They all help DAVIS to his feet. He is in a pitiful state, his whole head covered with oil and water. They sit him on the chair and CLIFTON picks up the helmet.)

VANCE. He smells like a Spanish pimp.

CONNIE. How do you know what a Spanish pimp smells like?

CLIFTON. I believe that would be the olive oil, sir.

CONNIE. How do you feel?

DAVIS. I think I might be a little discombobulated.

CONNIE. I think so too. Let's go in the kitchen and get you cleaned up.

DAVIS. *(Gets to his feet, groans and holds his head.)* Thank you, that would be nice.

(CONNIE and DAVIS exit to the kitchen.)

VANCE. Now Mr. Clifton, we never did finish our little chat did we?

CLIFTON. I suppose we didn't sir, tell you what, *(He is already moving U.L.)* let me just return this crowbar and I'll be right back.

(CLIFTON exits through the front door carrying the helmet and crowbar.)

VANCE. He's done it again.

(Enter RENEE from U.L.)

RENEE. Ah, Monsieur Vance, do you know where is Clifton?

VANCE. Yes, he's outside, he'll be back in a minute.

RENEE. *(Sees the trolley.)* Ooh—magnifique. I am, how you say in English, famished.

(She takes a plate and starts to put food on it.)

VANCE. Miss LaFleur, I'd like to talk to you about that check I gave you earlier.

RENEE. What is to talk? I sign the contract, you give me the check. C'est fini.

VANCE. Well it turns out it was a mistake.

RENEE. A very expensive mistake wouldn't you say?

VANCE. Well yes. That's the point.

RENEE. Monsieur Vance, I have this feeling that the contract was probably worked over and over by many lawyers to make quite sure it was iron-covered.

VANCE. Ironclad.

RENEE. Yes, of course, ironclad. This is so, n'est-ce-pas?

VANCE. This is so.

RENEE. Then, as you say in English, tough petunias!

(Enter CONNIE and DAVIS from the kitchen. He has a towel around

his shoulders, his face and hair cleaned up just a little. He is leaning on CONNIE and his legs keep buckling at the knees.)

CONNIE. Mr. Vance, could you give me a hand, his legs keep going out.

(VANCE comes L. to help support DAVIS.)

DAVIS. I'm so sorry, I seem to keep loosing my equilateral.

RENEE. *(Stands.)* Who is this?

VANCE. An apology for a detective.

CONNIE. I'm sure he is doing his best.

RENEE. Well he looks like, what is it you say in English? The dinner of the dog?

(Enter CLIFTON from the front door.)

CLIFTON. He looks terrible. Here, let's get him on the bed in my apartment. *(DAVIS, supported by CONNIE and VANCE, exits to the apartment as CLIFTON opens the door for them. He turns R. to RENEE.)* Ah, Miss Renee!

RENEE. *(Crosses L. to him.)* My beautiful Clifton. Now we are alone.

CLIFTON. *(Looks nervously around.)* We won't be for long.

(RENEE kisses him and he does not protest. SUSIE opens the kitchen door and stops in the doorway to watch.)

RENEE. *(Eventually.)* Ooh-la-la! You know, I opened the wine upstairs, it should have finished the breathing by now.

SUSIE. *(Steps into the room and comes between RENEE and CLIFTON.)* And I know someone who will also finish breathing if they don't leave my husband alone.

RENEE. Ooh-la-la, this is a feisty one. We shall see madame. Excusez-moi.

(She heads to the powder room.)

CLIFTON. Miss Renee, I wouldn't go—

SUSIE. *(Quickly interrupts him.)* Let her go, this should be fun.

(RENEE exits to the powder room and closes the door.)

CLIFTON. You don't like her, do you?

SUSIE. Not very much.

CLIFTON. What's wrong with her?

SUSIE. Well for a start, she could wear a longer skirt.

CLIFTON. Oh, I suppose you'd like to see her in a skirt that goes down to her ankles?

SUSIE. I'll bet the skirt she's got on is always down around her ankles!

(There is a scream from RENEE in the powder room. She rushes out hurriedly, closes the door behind her, then runs U.L. into the kitchen. SUSIE stands on the chair. CLIFTON looks at SUSIE, shrugs and follows RENEE into the kitchen. Enter AGNES from U.L.)

AGNES. Oscar, Oscar. *(She searches behind the sofa, then notices SUSIE standing on the chair.)* What are you doing up there?

SUSIE. You know very well what I'm doing up here.

AGNES. I said, What are you doing up there?

SUSIE. *(Shouts.)* You'd better switch it on.

AGNES. The bitch has gone? Which bitch has gone? *(SUSIE points to the switch and mouths "switch it on.")* Oh, alright then, just for a minute.

(She switches it on.
As SUSIE climbs down from the chair, VANCE appears in the apartment door just in time to hear:)

SUSIE. Agnes, I'll make a deal with you. If I tell you where Oscar is, will you promise to keep him out of the house the rest of the day.

(VANCE stays partially hidden by the apartment door listening.)

AGNES. You know where he is?
SUSIE. Yes.
AGNES. Where?
SUSIE. Promise?
AGNES. O.K. I promise.
SUSIE. He's in the powder room.

(VANCE reacts.)

AGNES. *(Rushes over to the powder room.)* Oscar, Oscar.

(She goes in leaving the door open, she reappears almost immediately cradling a bulge under her blouse. SUSIE jumps back up on the chair. AGNES closes the powder room door, smiles at SUSIE and exits out of the front door. SUSIE watches her go then exits to the kitchen.)

VANCE. *(Steps into the room.)* Well, well. Oscar, we've got you now my friend. *(He takes one of the bar stools, and crosses R. to wedge it under the powder room door handle.)* Time for a little backup I think.

(VANCE exits to the apartment.

Enter CLIFTON, SUSIE and RENEE from the kitchen. SUSIE is almost pushing CLIFTON into the room.)

SUSIE. If I catch you kissing that bimbo again—

RENEE. What is this word "bimbo"?

CLIFTON. It means—er—er—something like a beautiful woman.

RENEE. Ooh-la-la!

SUSIE. And you can stop "Ooh-la-la-ing".

CLIFTON. She was just showing her appreciation.

SUSIE. Oh, is that what she calls it?

(Enter VANCE, DAVIS and CONNIE from the apartment.)

VANCE. Excuse us. It's time for action.

CLIFTON. I beg your pardon?

VANCE. You ready, Davis?

DAVIS. *(Leaps all over the room doing his karate thing at various pieces of furniture.)* Ready.

CLIFTON. Excuse me, but what is going on here?

DAVIS. We are about to confront the penetrator of this bamboozlement.

CLIFTON. Bamboozlement?

CONNIE. He means embezzlement.

CLIFTON. Oh dear!

VANCE. *(He and DAVIS are now D.R. by the powder room door.)* Now here's how we'll do it. I'll pull the stool away and open the door, you get in there fast. O.K.?

DAVIS. O.K.

(DAVIS lines up about six feet L. of the door.)

CONNIE. Why do I get the feeling this is not going to work?

VANCE. Ready?

DAVIS. Ready. *(VANCE pulls the stool away and opens the door. DAVIS does his karate thing.)* Hi-ya!

(He leaps into the powder room, there is a huge thud and a crash. They watch the open door. After a brief pause, DAVIS staggers out. He has a toilet seat wedged under his right arm and the left side of his neck and a metal waste basket stuck on one foot.)

CONNIE. *(Rushes D.R. to help him.)* Oh you poor dear man.

VANCE. *(Looks in the powder room.)* He's not there, I don't understand. Davis you blithering idiot.

CONNIE. Mr. Vance, I've just about had enough. This poor creature has done his best, and all you can do is yell at him. I went along with your scheme to recover money from those people, but it must be obvious by now, even to a moron like you, that that's not going to happen. Please consider our business arrangement terminated.

VANCE. But Miss Olden—

CONNIE. —and kindly remove your presence from my house.

VANCE. But—

(CONNIE looks straight at him and points to the front door.)

DAVIS. *(To VANCE.)* It really wasn't my fault. I'm usually a very deficient detective.

VANCE. AAARGH!

(He heads to the front door, stops, then comes back down, seizes the painting off the wall, then exits out the front door.)

CONNIE. Come along, Mr. Davis. Let's get you upstairs. I think you really need someone to look after you.

DAVIS. You know, ever since I first saw you I found you very attractive.

CONNIE. Really?

DAVIS. Yes, I can see us together exploring erotic places.

CONNIE. *(Giggles)* You mean exotic don't you?

DAVIS. No!

CONNIE. Oh! *(They turn to go U.S. together and CONNIE bumps into the arm of the chair. She leaps back and does an elaborate karate kick at it.)* Hi-Ya!

(DAVIS smiles and gives her the "thumbs up" sign as they exit arm in arm U.R.)

RENEE. So Clifton, what is to become of us?

SUSIE. *(Stepping in between them.)* Nothing will become of you two. You, Miss LaFleur, will soon receive a substantial check, and my husband and I will then live happily ever after.

RENEE. This is so Clifton?

CLIFTON. Well—er—

SUSIE. Clifton!

CLIFTON. This is so.

RENEE. Do I at least get to kiss the lucky man?

SUSIE. I think you know what you can kiss!

(She puts her arm around CLIFTON.)

RENEE. Ah well. C'est la vie! We could have made beautiful music, Clifton. *(She goes to the front door, then turns and strikes a sexy pose.)* Ooh-la-la.

(RENEE exits through the front door.)

CLIFTON. *(Looks wistfully after her.)* I suppose it's for the best.

(Takes SUSIE's hands in his.) I shall miss you.

(They lean ever closer to each other. When their lips are about one inch apart, SUSIE stops.)

SUSIE. Were you going to kiss me, Clifton?
CLIFTON. Well—er—I don't know.
SUSIE. Did you want to?
CLIFTON. Well. *(He pauses and looks at her.)* Oh yes!
SUSIE. Very well, let's get one or two things straight. My job as an actress is over, however, *(They walk slowly to the kitchen.)* you may take me out for dinner this evening, but I expect you to behave like a gentleman. There will be no touching of any kind, I do not kiss until the third date, and even then—

(They exit to the kitchen.)

CURTAIN

AUTHOR'S NOTES

If, as was intended by the author, the roles of Josephine, Renee and Marjorie are played by the same actress, then a substitute would be required for the following:

pages 50-54	Josephine's arm, head, legs, etc.
page 59	The back of Marjorie's head and body.
page 61	Josephine's arm.
page 65	Josephine's arm.
page 79	Josephine's hands.
pages 86-90	Josephine's legs
page 101	Josephine's arm
page 86	If a duplicate trolley can be made, to be waiting with the substitute's legs ready in the powder room, the changeover can be make in a second or two. If not, the time needed for Josephine to dismount from the trolley and the substitute to take her place would obviously be a few seconds longer.

FURNITURE AND PROPERTY LIST

ONSTAGE

Oil painting
Table with wine glasses, corkscrews, wine bottles and bar paraphernalia
Table with flowers, ornaments and bric-a-brac
Sofa
Coffee table
Low-back easy chair
2 bar stools
Built-in bar
On it: telephone, pen, checkbook
Behind it: wine racks, bottles, glasses, etc.

ACT I — OFFSTAGE

Tray with coffee pot, cups, etc. (Agnes)
Suitcase (Josephine)
Wine bottle (Agnes)
Suitcase (Renee)
Bucket and mop, etc. (Agnes)
Dish towel (Clifton)
Underwear ("Josephine")
Suitcase (Marjorie)

ACT II — OFFSTAGE

Wine bottle (Renee)
Serving trolley with dishes, large bowl with salad, silver platter, sandwiches, olive oil, vinegar
Vacuum cleaner (Agnes)
Mop (Agnes)
Covered dish (Susie)

Broom (Marjorie)
Champagne bottle (Clifton)
Wine bottle (Josephine)
Champagne bottle with ice bucket (Susie)
Armored helmet (Davis)
Crowbar (Clifton)
Towel (Davis)
Toilet seat (Davis)
Wastebasket (Davis)

PERSONAL

Hearing aid (Agnes)
Feather duster (Agnes)
Purse (Susie)
Pen and contract (Susie)
Briefcase with files, papers, check, pen (Vance)
Cell phone (Vance)
Briefcase (Davis)
Wrist chain (Davis)
Umbrella (Davis)
Business card (Davis)
Notebook and pencil (Davis)
Cell phone (Davis)

COSTUMES

AGNES
Skirt
Blouse with pockets
Hose
Shoes

CLIFTON
White shirt
Bow tie
Vest
Dark pants
Dress shoes

SUSIE
Pastel linen suit
Silk blouse
Hose
Slip
High heel pumps
Wig
Glasses
Pregnancy padding
Maternity dress
Flat shoes
Spare bra

CONNIE
Long- sleeve dress
Hose
Flat shoes

VANCE
Dark business suit
Shirt and tie
Dress shoes
Hat

JOSEPHINE
Lightweight summer suit
with bolero jacket
Blouse
Hose
High heels
Bed sheet wrap around

WILLIAM DAVIS JR.
Sport coat
Dress pants
Dress shirt
Socks
Shoes
Yellow smiley face
boxers

RENEE
Blouse
Tailored skirt
Hose
High heels

MARJORIE
Halter top
Mini skirt
Flat what sandals

SET DRAWING

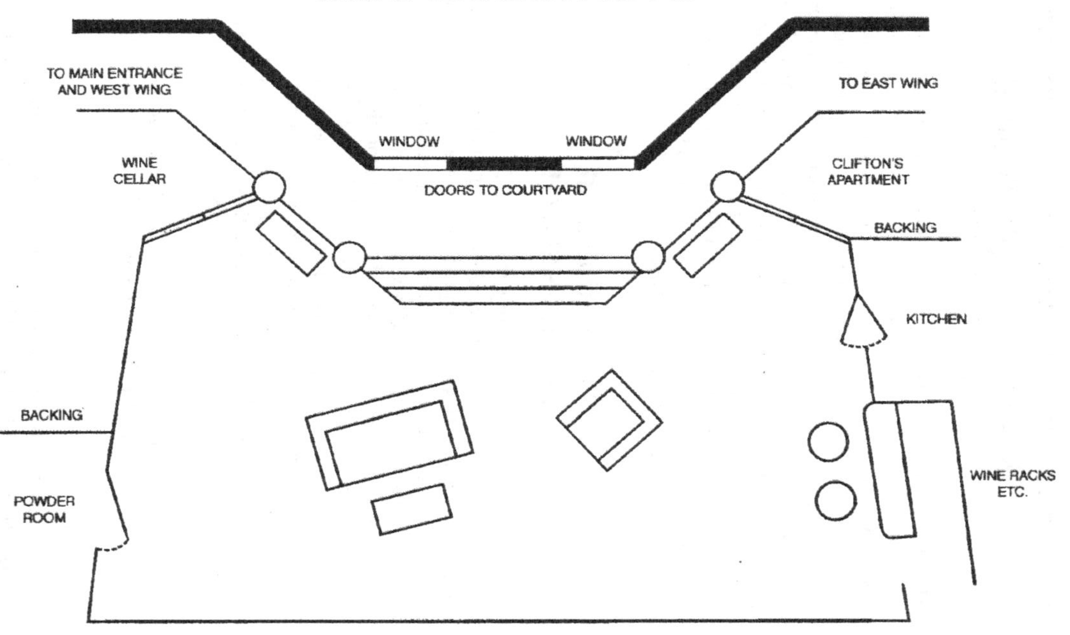
TO MAIN ENTRANCE
AND WEST WING
WINDOW
WINDOW
TO EAST WING
WINE
CELLAR
DOORS TO COURTYARD
CLIFTON'S
APARTMENT
BACKING
KITCHEN
BACKING
POWDER
ROOM
WINE RACKS
ETC.